The Displacers

MEAGAN 3

By T. M. Baker

This is a work of Fiction. Names, characters and incidents are either the product of the author's imagination or are used fictitiously and resemblance to actual persons, living or dead or locales is entirely coincidental.

Copyright © 2021 by **T. M. Baker**

BookBaby
7905 North Crescent Boulevard
Pennsauken, NJ 08110
www.BookBaby.com

Ordering Information:
For details, contact **distribution@bookbaby.com**.

Print ISBN: 9781667815961
eBook ISBN: 9781667815978

Printed in the United States of America on SFI Certified paper.

First Edition

Acknowledgments

Devon- for always supporting my ideas and pushing me to never give up on them.

Nicki- for her help in refocusing this story as well as her support in proof reading and editing. Though I did add a lot more content afterwards…oops.

My mom- who constantly said that I could do anything that I put my mind to. That is if I would just stop procrastinating.

And a special thanks to Kyle Small and the rest of the guys from Split Shift for the use of the lyrics to their song "Forget"

Key-Legend

" " : Regular Quotation Marks-used when voices are speaking aloud.

≈ ≈ : Mental Quotation Marks-used when people are communicating via a Mental Lync.

~ ~ : Single Mental Quotation Mark-used when someone is thinking to themselves, when talking to themselves or having a conversation with themselves in their head.

¥ ¥: Music/Song lyrics-being heard, sung or played.

PROLOGUE

It's nighttime outside a military installation code named
"GF1". Guards were on patrol inside and outside of the facility.
There was a large gravity fence surrounding the grounds.
Though the fence could not be seen by the naked eye, the signs
floating on them could. They read:

Facility One
No un-escorted entry allowed!
No Lyncing {link-ing} beyond this point!!
Lyncing beyond this point may result in permanent
&
Severe mental trauma!

Out of nowhere, alarms began going off. Lights lit up the
outside the facility. Guards began running around. Vehicle
doors could be heard closing as engines began to start. Guns
could be heard being locked and loaded. Suddenly there was a
bright white flash then nothing. Silence fell over the entire
facility.

Miles away, at the Central Security Office (CSO), the
alarms had registered and systems began showing a strange
code on most of the screens. The security office personnel

began to scramble around the room trying to figure out the source of the alarm and error message.

The CSO was the center of all information in the five galaxies. Every bit of information flowed through this office. Whether it was how tall the grass grew on a particular planet to who's military had the most destructive weapons and where they were being hid.

A few minutes later there was a knock at a door. The sound of someone speaking a strange language could be heard coming from inside the room. The door opened and the head of the CSO appeared.

"What is it?" he yelled.

It had been a long day and he had just started to fall asleep when the knock occurred.

"Sorry, sir but we have an issue with the system," The officer said shakily.

The head of the CSO was not known for his warmth. And even though they were members of the same species, the officer knew that wouldn't be enough for him to get on his good side.

"An alarm went off but we can't seem to find the source of it." The officer said.

"Do you know how to do your job?" The head officer asked.

"Do I need to hold your pale blue hands and show you what to do?"

"No sir, but an error message came up, locking most of the systems and no one seems to know what it is or how to…"

He was interrupted by the head officer.

"What error message?" he asked.

"The screens say DSU-0."

The head officer's blue skin began to turn grey, which made his junior officer nervous. They were from a planet mainly comprised of water. Their skin was naturally blue. The longer they were out of water the more their skin would lighten up slightly but it only turned grey when there was a serious chemical imbalance. And extreme fear can definitely cause that.

As his color slowly began to change back, he said, "Type in CMJ-1. That should release the system. Then notify the Council."

The officer, still a little shaky said, "You want me to wake the Council?"

"I'm sorry, did you not understand me?" The Head Officer rebuffed.

He then said something in his native language which loosely translated to, "Do you really want to die right now?"

"No sir," The Junior Officer said.

He then turned and quickly headed back to the CSO.

The head officer slowly closed his door. Realizing that he probably wouldn't be able to get any sleep anytime soon, he filled his tub up with water and just submerged himself for awhile.

Chapter 1

Time: Over twenty solar cycles ago. Aka 20 years.

Place: Meagan 3. A system with seven planets where the third and forth planet were set in a duel orbit separated by a single moon between them.

Last officially sanctioned mission for DSU-1. (Displacers Special Unit)

A large battle cruiser begins its descent into Meagan 3's upper atmosphere.

On the surface, inside their planetary defense bunker, the Grand Chancellor was meeting with his top general. Also present was Specialist Keller, a member of DSU-1.

"So, why isn't there a peace envoy en route to meet them?" The Chancellor asked.

"Because, I doubt they're here to negotiate." The General answered.

"Specialist Keller, what do you think?" The Chancellor asked turning towards her.

"Well Chancellor," she responded, "we were sent here just to observe, not to really advise you on what to do. But unofficially, if the Veagans {vay-gans} are landing a battle cruiser on any inhabited planet, odds are that it's not going to be good."

"Well what about Commander Johnson? What does he think?" The Chancellor asked then paused adding. "By the way, where is he?"

"He said he was doing a last minute check of the perimeter." She then tapped her wrist twice and called Commander Johnson.

"Commander, where are you?" she asked.

"Oh hey Sis," Commander Johnson replied. "Kent said he saw something, so we're just doing a quick sweep."

"Did you notice the large battle cruiser about to land?" She asked.

"Yeah looks real nice from this angle. But don't worry. We'll be back long before they make landfall," He replied.

Kent and the Commander were making their way through a thickly settled area, filled with trees and heavy brush. As they continued they noticed that the area seemed to have opened up but in fact it was the trees that had changed. They went from an area full of green and brightly colored leaves to an area with no leaves at all. The trees and brush were a silver-grayish color and the bushes were nothing but sticks. The only sound seemed to be that of sticks and branches crunching beneath their feet. It was like going from a color movie to black and white.

"Commander," Kent said. "Did you have to tell Specialist Keller that it was my idea to check out this area?"

"Well," the Commander answered, "When you're a part of a Displacers Unit you have to take the good with the bad. And telling her that, well, that's good for me and kind of bad for you." The Commander smiled.

"Now where is this place you said that you noticed?" He asked.

Kent pointed to an area up and to the right of their position, where the outline of a grayish building could be seen. As they approached a fence, they noticed that there were no security measures in place. There was no gate and no vehicles could be seen. The Commander motioned Kent to circle around the right side of the building and the Commander took the left and the rear. Raising his plasma rifle, Kent looked through the scope scanning the different spectrums as he headed around the building. Kent was the first to return from his sweep. As the Commander was coming into view, Kent could hear that he was having trouble communicating with the ship.

"Sorry," Kent said. "I guess it was nothing after all. It did look like there was a security office behind that door but I couldn't find anything else on any spectrum."

The Commander tried to reach the ship but communication was sporadic.

≈Crystal? ≈ The Commander thought. ≈Are you there? ≈

≈Yes,≈ She replied.

≈What's up with our communication? ≈ He asked.

≈I'm having trouble connecting with the ship. Not sure why but it seems that the closer we get to this structure, the more our communication with the ship is disrupted. Seems to be some kind of major electronic shielding coming from over there.≈ she replied.

"Well Kent," The Commander said.

"Looks like you may be on to something. You said that you got no readings when you checked your scope? Is that correct?" The Commander asked.

"Yes. Nothing showed up." Kent replied.

"Well that's odd, since Crystal says the communication disturbance is coming from in there. Guess we'll take a quick look inside."

They headed slowly though the front door and entered a small foyer. They proceeded through a second set of doors and felt as if they were in an entirely different building. The entire hallway was white from floor to ceiling. Even the security booth was entirely white, inside and out. The corridor looked to be a couple hundred feet long, but that could have been an optical illusion because of the color. At the end of the corridor there was a wall with a panel on either side of it. Both were white with clear buttons on them. In between the panels on the floor was a light outline of two shoe prints.

Kent stopped in the security booth and had a look around while the Commander continued down the hallway. There was an opening to the office but no physical door. There was enough room for maybe 3 or 4 individuals inside the booth. The booth contained two desks, one facing the outside door and the other faced the corridor. Each desk had three monitors on top of them, with multiple keyboards. There was a chair on each side and large windows behind each monitor.

"Do you think Specialist Keller will be ok if we're late?" Kent asked.

"She'll be fine and we won't be late," The Commander replied.

The Commander had been on plenty of missions with Specialist Keller and he knew that she could handle herself in almost any situation. She was very knowledgeable of most cultures and could negotiate with the most difficult of species. Besides, she had dealt with the Commander for many years now and if she could deal with him, then she could deal with anyone. The Commander remembered when Specialist Keller joined his team. She only had three requests. First: no getting friendly with the natives. Second: no picking up strays. And third was...

"Commander!" Kent shouted. "This is strange. The monitors all show that they are powered up but the vids are all black."

"No," The Commander responded.

"What's strange is that the monitors are only focused on the interior of this building and not one shows the outside of it. What's strange is that drink on the desk has hot liquid in it but there's no other sign of life here."

Kent looked down by his hand and wondered how he hadn't noticed the large amount of steam coming off of the cup.

The Commander continued.

"But what's really strange is that there seems to be an Anti Veagan Security System set up at the end of this corridor."

"What?" Kent said curiously as he popped his head up from the monitors. Kent hurried out of the security booth and headed towards the Commander.

"How can you tell?" Kent asked.

"This is only a theory but I overheard someone talking about a system that closely resembles this. It was a discussion about how they would make an anti-Veagan system, if the opportunity came up. It involved a thick almost impenetrable door, with panels on either side. One panel would be for an optical/retina scanner. The other would be some sort of hand print/DNA analyzer. Lastly, there would be a beam that would encompass and lift up the person in a zero gravity bubble. It would then run a molecule scan on the subject. While you were lifted up, the floor would open up to reveal anything from, spikes, acid, poison gas etc… The best part was that none of the systems would let you know if you failed. So you wouldn't know if you failed until after the gravity bubble burst and dropped you in the pit or gently placed you back on the floor."

Kent started to move ahead of the Commander to where the shoe outline on the floor was. But the Commander quickly reached out his hand to stop him.

"This may only be a theory," the Commander said. "But once you get close enough to the system it automatically starts up. And once it does there's no stopping it."

Kent stopped and said.

"But you're not sure if that's what we're dealing with here, right?"

"No," the Commander replied while turning slowly to Kent.

"But do you want to take that chance? We'll just have to find another way in."

As they headed back past the security booth, the Commander asked if Kent found any other entrances while doing his sweep outside. Kent shook his head no. Once through the door something slowly appeared on the monitor. It was small and had a greenish glow surrounding it. It appeared from the bottom left hand of the screen, briefly stopped, then slowly moved back off the screen.

The two headed towards the left hand side of the building where the Commander had been earlier. The Commander seemed to be looking for something; he then said.
"Yeah, this should do."

Reaching down into a side pocket, the Commander pulled out a device that Kent didn't recognize. It was rectangular in shape and a couple of inches thick. It had a small screen near the top and a few square buttons underneath. He headed toward the front door, stopped. Then using the device, he took a picture of the door and headed back. The Commander turned the device over. Kent noticed that near each corner were little round bumps. The Commander then peeled off a thin, clear protective covering from each of them and held the device against the wall. He then punched in a 4 digit code and the device began burrowing into the wall until it was flush. The Commander touched the screen and scrolled to the picture he just took, punched in a three digit code and stood back.
"What is that?" Kent asked.

A section of the wall began to ripple, as if a stone was dropped into a pond.
The Commander said, "It's a VGND1."

The wall rippled again as Kent looked at the Commander with a puzzled look.

"I know," the Commander said.

"It's really not a cool name but I've been trying to come up with one since I first got a hold of this device. And that's all I got so far."

The wall rippled again, a little faster this time.

"It's a prototype for a portable door," the Commander said.

"A portable door?" Kent asked.

"Yeah." The Commander responded. "You know that the Veagans are mercenaries know for being first rate in espionage and assassinations."

"Yes, because they're a race of shape shifters." Kent said.

"Correct." The Commander nodded.

"We know that they can imitate anything organic and it's been long speculated that they can imitate anything inorganic as well. So, Dr. Z came up with this little toy. It uses Veagan DNA to change the surrounding structure to the one pictured on the screen, thus a VGND1."

Again, Kent gave the Commander a strange look.

"No?" the Commander asked.

"Then how about A Veagan door then?"

"Maybe you should just stick to portable door." Kent said.

The Commander sighed. The wall had been rippling faster and faster as they spoke. Then as the rippling began to slow, the wall changed appearance. It now resembled the door on the front of the building. Once the rippling stopped, the Commander turned to Kent.

"Hopefully I picked the right spot." The Commander said as he reached out his hand and pushed.

The door slowly opened. It looked like the Commander picked the perfect spot. The door opened on a wall inside a corridor. The corridor stretched out to the left of them, with rooms on the right hand side and two double doors at the end. The double doors had little round windows near the tops of them, and both were totally dark. The corridor was brightly lit which made it easier to see inside the rooms. The first was a lab, with large glass windows from floor to ceiling. The rest of the rooms had doors with windows in them. As they walked towards the lab, the door swung closed behind them and rippled slightly. It also revealed a wall to the right of the portable door.

The Commander told Kent that they needed to look for a working terminal to try to figure out what was going on here as quickly as possible. He emphasized that they did not have time to look through the whole place. Inside the lab, they found most of the equipment running automatically. Mechanical arms were moving vials around. Test tubes were shaking and spinning on various machines. But they couldn't find any terminals to plug into. So they moved to the next room which was almost in total darkness. The power to that room seemed to have been cut off. It was in the third room where they found what they were looking for. A terminal in the corner of the room which could possibly give them access to what they needed. As the Commander looked it over, he instructed Kent to keep an eye on their portable door. Being a prototype, the Commander wasn't 100% sure how long it would last.

≈Crystal? ≈The Commander thought. ≈Are you still there? ≈

≈Yes.≈ she responded.

≈Are you able to access this terminal? ≈ He asked

≈No.≈ she responded. ≈The electronic interference in here is too strong for me to link up to it. But if you brought my extra node along, you can plug it into the terminal and then I should be able to link up to it.≈

≈Good.≈ He responded.

The Commander then pulled her node from his pocket and plugged it into the terminal and she began scanning the system.

Outside Kent was watching the doors at the end of the corridor. He would periodically turn to watch the portable door but he was drawn to the doors at the end of the corridor. Then, out the corner of his eye, Kent thought he saw something move behind those doors.

"Commander!" Kent yelled. "I think I saw movement!"

"Is the door starting to ripple?" The Commander asked.

"No. I thought I saw something at the other end of the corridor." Kent said.

"I'm gonna go check it out."

"Negative." The Commander said.

"I'm almost done scanning through the files and we don't have time for that. Your only job right now is to watch our exit." The Commander said never once looking up from the monitor.

While Crystal was scanning through the terminal, videos were flashing across the screen.

≈Was that just…? ≈ the Commander thought as the last video flashed by.

≈Yes.≈ Crystal responded.

"I'm going to kill him." the Commander said angrily

≈But more importantly≈ Crystal said.

≈I think Lieutenant. Kent has left his post.≈

"Damn!" the Commander said as he looked up from the monitor and towards the door.

Kent had made his way down the hall to the double doors. He tried to look through the windows but they were too dark to see through. He took a step back and tried using the scope on his plasma rifle but he couldn't make out anything. So he turned on the light at the end of his weapon and slowly, using the end of his rifle, he pushed the door open on his left.

Starting with the floor then slowly moving his weapon upwards, Kent began scanning through the room. He saw desks and chairs in the darkness but not much else. Kent checked behind the door and then slowly let it close behind him. But he still didn't see anything. As he took another step he felt something grab his leg. Kent nearly jumped out of his skin. As he pointed his weapon downward, he heard a very soft voice. "Help me." It said.

The light at the end of his rifle showed a hand on his ankle. It was attached to a female wearing a white lab coat. She was lying on the floor under a desk.

"Are you alright?" Kent asked.

"What happened?"

But all she could say was "Help me."

Kent bent down to help the woman up but because he was behind the desk, he didn't notice the little glowing orbs that were stating to move from the back of the room towards them. Kent slung his rifle over his right shoulder. He then grabbed and put her right arm around his neck and over his shoulder. He then put his left arm under her left armpit and hoisted her up and began to drag her through the double doors. For some reason she was a lot heavier than she looked. As he struggled to drag her body down the corridor, he could hear the Commander yelling at him.

"Kent!" The Commander yelled.

"What are you doing?"

"Sir, I thought I saw something. Then I found this scientist underneath a desk back there."

"Kent, didn't I say to watch the door, and that we didn't have time to search this place?" He asked.

"Yes Sir But…"

Kent's answer was interrupted by the sound of a plasma rifle being charged. Kent could feel the hairs on his arm starting to stand on end. He also felt as if the temperature in the corridor had suddenly tripled. As he looked up, in that single moment, Kent realized that he had never had a plasma rifle pointed at him before. Not in the over 70 missions he had been on. Not during his training and never by a commanding officer. But as he saw the coils of the plasma rifle began to glow, Kent knew that the Commander wouldn't shoot. He was in the right, no matter what the Commander had asked him to do. And even though Specialist Keller had a few rules that she liked the team to follow, he knew that she would back him up. Just then Kent felt as if the left side of his body had suddenly burst into flames. Then he felt something wet splash on his face. And as he slowly looked down and to the left, he realized that her head was now gone. The shot had not only splattered it on the wall, the door and Kent but it had instantly cauterized the wound.

Kent fell to the floor in shock, which is why he couldn't hear the Commander yelling at him to get up. As he stared at her lifeless body, his body still felt as if it was on fire. It wasn't until the second shot went by him that Kent started to slowly come back to reality. He could just start to hear the Commander say that he was going to leave him behind if he didn't get a move on. As Kent started to get up, the woman's body slowly slumped to the floor. That's when Kent noticed his wrist was flashing Yellow with Red lettering scrolling across it. **"Viral Proximity Warning."** This made Kent move a little faster but he almost fell again because the female scientist's left hand was clutching onto Kent's pant leg. As Kent tried to regain his balance something started to emerge from her body. Three small oblong orbs, about six to eight inches each, began to come out of her body. Kent was able to kick her hand off of his pants leg and, using his rife like a walking stick, he was able to regain his balance and make his way toward the Commander. Before Kent had reached the exit, the orbs had fully emerged from her body and stopped about two feet above it. They were light yellow in color and still seemed to be attached to the body by a two foot long umbilical cord, which almost looked as if they were pulsing. They soon realized that what looked like pulsing was actually the orbs feeding, sucking something out of her body. After each small pulse the orb slightly changed color. From light yellow to yellow, yellow to light green, then light green to bright green. In between each color change something could be seen moving inside the orb. It looked like a small fetus of sorts. Right before it turned light green, Kent had managed to push through the door with the Commander not far behind them. They ran towards the field. About halfway to the fence line, the Commander moved his pulse rifle to his left hand. Then drawing his side arm with his right, and turning slightly to his left, he fired three quick pulses toward the door. The second one found its mark, hitting the VGN panel almost dead center, shattering it to pieces so small that it almost totally disintegrated.

The door pulsed and then began to ripple very quickly. The Commander returned his gun into its holster and continued towards their ship. He had quickly passed Kent and was about six paces ahead of him when they heard a loud shrill and a dull popping sound coming from behind them. Back at the portable door, between the third and fourth rippling of the door, the first orb slipped through. The second slipped through between the fifth and sixth pulses. The third was just starting to emerge after the eighth pulse when the door suddenly vanished and the wall solidified with the third orb halfway through. The creature inside began to shrill right before the orb popped. Green liquid, along with half of the creature's body, began to ooze down the side of the wall until it slowly hit the ground. Its color began to fade and it eventually turned grey. The ooze turned black and a black mist could be seen rising up from it into the air.

Tapping his left wrist twice, the Commander spoke. "Crystal! Crystal, are you there?" He yelled.

"Yes, I'm still here." She replied.

"Prep the ship. We're coming in hot and need to dust off immediately." He said.

"Roger that." She said as the ship's engines began to start up.

"Hey Nicki, can you hear me?" the Commander asked after double tapping his wrist again.

Specialist Keller knew something was wrong if the Commander was calling her Nicki during a mission.

"Yes," she replied.

"Did you find something?" she asked.

As the Commander began to answer, she could hear what sounded like plasma rifles going off in the background.

"Well, looks like we ran into a small situation out here and we'll be heading your way very shortly," he said.

"I hope you're not out there getting friendly with the natives again?" She asked.

"Well if these are the natives then we're in…" The Commander's voice was cut off by a sudden "BOOM!"

Followed by what sounded like lightning striking dry trees. Then she heard, "CRACKLE!", then a dull "Pop". "Crackle, crackle, crackle, pop." Then the crackling sound slowly faded away.

"Commander?" she said inquisitively.

"Did you just use a Plasma Grenade?"

"Ummm, no...no I didn't. But I think Kent may have," He replied.

"Ok what's going…"

"Sorry." The Commander interrupted.

"But I'm declaring a Category Three Omega Level threat. Tell the Meagans that they have about 30 minutes to evacuate the planet."

The Commander could hear the Chancellor in the background yelling that they had no authority to do that. That they never signed the Pelham Accord, so they had no authority to use that protocol on their planet.

"Sis, can you deal with that?" The Commander asked.

"I'm sure the Veagans have made landfall by now, so stay in the command center until we arrive. We'll signal you to come out when we arrive."

"Ok, I understand." she replied. "Just be safe."

"Always." The Commander said.

"See ya in a bit."

Specialist Keller then turned and began to deal with the Chancellor. Kent and the Commander had made it to their ship. Once inside, they began to lift off and head towards Specialist Keller's location.

The cockpit had room for five but the Commander had removed two of the seats, since there were only three of them on this mission.

The Commander sat in the seat on the left, Kent the one on the right, and the one behind them would be for Specialist Keller. The Commander touched the console and spoke. "This is Commander T.M. Johnson DSU1. I'm declaring an Omega Level threat on Meagan Three."

The computer responded. "Is this Omega Level threat confirmed? Remember, once confirmed this order cannot be rescinded."

Kent was having trouble catching his breath but managed to say. "This is Lieutenant R. Kent DSUr1, confirming Omega Level threat."

"Omega Level threat confirmed." The computer responded. "What category?"

"Category three," The Commander responded.

"Category three confirmed. You now have thirty minutes until Omega Level Protocol is activated," the computer said.

The Commander, Specialist Keller and Lieutenant Kent's wrist all light up with a 30 minute timer beginning the countdown. Kent looked at the Commander and said, "I'm sorry. You were right. I should have not disobeyed you orders."

But the Commander didn't respond. He was looking at Kent's wrist. Kent looked down and noticed his wrist was flashing red with black words scrolling across.

"D A N G E R.... C O N T A M I N A T I O N!!!"

Just then Kent noticed that the hairs on his arm had begun to stand on end. And as he slowly looked up, he thought, ~This is now the second time I've had a Plasma Rifle pointed at.......~

Key-Definitions

CSO: Central Security Office- Room where all information from surrounding galaxies are collected.

Note: (It would be known as the hub of the intelligence community, if they actually shared their information with the rest of the universe.)

DSU: Displacers Special Unit- Teams made up of five members. Each team is assigned a mission or they travel throughout the galaxies to try to confirm and or prevent any Displacers incursion.

MLP: Mental Lync Percentage- How much of one's mental ability is able to be used.

MHV: Military Hover Vehicle-Vehicles that actually hover about 3-4 feet off the ground. These vehicles can only be operated mentally. So only species with a high MLP are allowed to operate these. **Note**: (Because of this fact there are only a few Civilian Hover Vehicles on the entire planet.)

Plasma Rifle: Standard weapon for the DSU. Uses heated plasma blast which can melt through most metals or even be used to surgically cut off a specific body part.(if the need arises)

NLC/MLC: Neuro Lync Cutter/Mental Lync Cutter-weapon which sends a pulse strong enough to sever any mental lync. **Note**: (This weapon has been banned because of the unavoidable and sometime severe side effects. Also nick named "**The Nite-Nite Gun**")

Plasma Whip: Whip that when used sends a plasma charge out of the tip when it comes in contact with any object. **Note**: (This weapon gives off a lot of heat since it is always charged, so very few species are capable of using it)

NGZ-301: Negative Zero Bomb- An Omega Level device used to sanitize a planet by reducing it to a temperature of negative zero to the three hundredth and first degree.

Plasma Grenade: Grenade which shoots out heated plasma in the form of "bolts of lightning" in a 360* radius. **Note**: (Sometimes referee to as "Little Medusa")

Pulse Canons: large planetary weapons which uses invisible pulses of energy to deter or destroy approaching enemy ships in orbit.

Quarantine: Stationary ship in orbit where anyone who has been off world, for 7 days or longer, has to be kept until decontamination procedures is done. **Note**: (This does not apply to the DSU. Not only do their ships contain this procedure but their Physical Lyncs allows the central computer to monitor their vitals at all times.)

Displacers: The most feared race in the entire universe. Origins unknown, name unknown. For many years none who encountered them lived to tell the tale. But for those who were off world when they arrived and returned after they had left, to them they would come to be known as "The Displacers"

Chapter II

As the ship takes off, the crackling sound of a pulse rifle can be heard echoing throughout the ship.

The ship turned one hundred and eighty degrees then headed off towards Specialist Keller's location. As the facility began shrinking in the distance, something could be seen falling from the ship. Just then the Commander woke up. Slowly sitting up, he put his hand on his head. Then moving his legs over the edge of the bed he sat there for a while.

≈You had that dream about our last mission again, didn't you? ≈ Crystal asked.

"You know it's illegal to lync into someone's dreams. I could report you for that," The Commander said.

She knew he was just being cranky as usual, being so early in the morning and all.

≈Yes, I know. ≈ She replied.

"So what's on today's schedule?" He asked.

≈Well first orange juice. Then a little exercise followed by relaxing out in the yard. ≈

"Wait, orange juice?" he questioned.

"It's supposed to be navel juice this morning."

≈ Unfortunately we ran out of navel juice. If orange juice isn't ok, then you can always have Andorian berry juice. ≈

The Commander didn't really care for Andorian berry juice and he thought orange juice was just a watered down version of navel juice. But if it was all he had on hand, then it would have to do.

Inside the council chambers, the councilors could be heard loudly discussing the recent events at GF1.

The council was made up of twelve members, most of whom were just ordinary citizens who survived the Displacers invasion of their worlds. They were in charge of creating laws that would protect the planet, though they still needed a majority of the voters to make it binding. Only items concerning the military and anything regarding the Displacers did not require the approval of the people.

A teacher's voice can be heard asking questions to her class as a green field can be seen through the window of the classroom.

There is a large hill off in the distance with a small structure barely visible a little farther away. On the front of the building, in large words is "Orientation and Interplanetary Education." Underneath this was a digital sign that said the same thing but it was rotating between multiple languages.

"What is "Lyncing?" The teacher asked.

"Lyncing is the ability to lync one's mind to someone else's or to a computer. It takes a while to learn but almost everyone in our society has the ability to some extent." A young student replied.

"Correct." She said.

"Now can anyone tell me how many levels of lyncing there are and what they are called?"

Another student said,

"There are three levels. Non-Lyncers who can only use ten to nineteen percent of their brain capacity. Regular Lyncers who can use twenty to eighty four percent of their mental capacity and Pure Lyncers who can use eighty five to one hundred percent of their mental capacity."

"Correct" adding,

"Most of us will fall into the regular lyncers category. A few will fall into the non-lyncing category, which can be a highly sought after group. Non-lyncers are usually hired by people and companies who want to create something new without the worry of someone mentally leaking their product too soon. And pure lyncers, as everyone knows, are the most sought after group there is. Pure lyncers can do almost anything. This planet and solar system were created by pure lyncers. Using the cocoon located at the planets core, they used their combined mental abilities to gather space dust and other debris to surround it thus creating this planet. And now, at the center of this planet, pure lyncers are at this very moment controlling the entire planet. From planetary rotation, to the temperature and how much oxygen is in the air, down to the length of the grass."

A security camera enters through the front door of the education facility. It continues down the hall and into the first door on the left. There we find former Specialist Nicole "Nicki" Keller aka "Sis" retired, now known as Mrs. Smith. She is in charge of the largest education facility on the planet. She stood about 5'5", had shoulder length dirty blond hair and light hazel blue eyes.

"Ok, who can tell me what Quarantine is"? She asked.

Desks begin to light up and Mrs. Smith picks a student. "Quarantine is what everyone who has either never been on the planet or who has been away from the planet for more than seven days has to go through. They are kept in a special ship, in orbit and then tested to make sure they are not Veagans or Displacers." A child student said.

"Correct. We use the quarantine system to make sure we are kept safe at all times."

Back at the council chambers, the meeting is now over and only councilor Price remains. Price has been the head of the planetary council since it was formed. A former member of

Recon 15, he was especially qualified to deal with most of the problems that arose here.

He was a tall, dark skinned man. And the only way that people knew that he was slightly older than most was because of the grey hairs that had started to appear on his head, which he didn't have much of.

Recon 15 was one of many recon units that used to patrol the five galaxies. Their mission: to be a first warning system to a Displacers attack. But like many, they usually would end up encountering the enemy as it was attacking an unsuspecting civilization. The team would then have to defend the planet until the population had escaped. Or at least long enough so some of them could.

Price was reading over a file when Lieutenant Heart walked into the council chambers. As she stood there, he did not immediately acknowledge her. As she was waiting to be noticed, she realized that Price was not as dark as she thought. She had heard that all of Recon 15 had dark skin but his was relatively lighter than she thought. But then again, compared to her yellowish skin she guessed he would be considered dark. "I was just going over your file. Top marks during training, set records in multiple courses and was the first female of any species to pass Luccardi's special training. Congratulations." He said adding.

"But now it seems like you've been demoted and are serving two consecutive suspensions. So can you tell me why that is? "

"Well you have my file right there." Lieutenant Heart said.

"Yes but sometimes the files don't tell the whole story."

"Well my commanding officer had made unwanted advances towards me and he didn't like when I said no. So during my last mission, he tried to force himself on me and I defended myself." She responded.

"I guess so. It says here that it'll take him two months before he can leave the infirmary. And for that you were put on six months suspension and demoted. So, what about the incident with the training instructor." Price asked.

"He heard about what had happened during that mission and decided to take revenge for my commanding officer during our training session. So again I defended myself." She said.

"And he'll be in the infirmary for at least five months." Price said,

"oh and just an FYI, that instructor was your commanding officer's father."

Lieutenant Heart just smiled and said,

"I know."

"Well I'm sure that that fact was why they considered it a training accident and only added six months to your suspension and not another demotion. But I might be able to help with that."

"Well I'm sorry if one of them is a friend of yours, but I don't plan on apologizing." She said stubbornly

"Actually I was thinking of offering you a special mission with automatic reinstatement if you accepted. I'd also wipe these last couple of incidents off your record at the successful completion of said mission. You interested?" He asked.

"What's the mission?" She asked curiously.

"Well because of the sensitive nature, I'm not allowed to go into details until you accept it. But I can say that during this mission you will be granted temporary Omega Level status."

Omega Level status was usually only given to members of the DSU or a special ops mission but never to regular military personnel and never to just one person. So she could assume that she would be a part of a team if she accepted. That could even be enough to get her into the DSU.

"Ok, I'm in," she said.

And with that Councilor Price started to go over the mission details. There were three parts to the mission. First: Deliver a message along with Intel on last night's incident to Commander Johnson. Second: Convince Commander Johnson to meet with Councilor Price. Third would be disclosed once the first two parts were completed. After filling her with much needed knowledge about how to deal with the Commander,

Price tossed a patch with the omega symbol on it before sending her to medical to get her military lync.

"Make sure to put this on your uniform after you go to medical," Price said, adding. "After the incident on Atavus, the Commander has had lyncing issues. So make sure to get a hard copy of last night's incident from CSO (Central Security Office) before heading out."

Lieutenant Heart then turned and left the council chambers and headed to medical where they gave her a military lync.

Physical Lyncs were used when mental lyncing was unavailable. But for military personnel, physical lyncs were crucial. Not only to help team members keep in contact when separated but it also let the central computer monitor their vitals as well. Comprised of a clear bio-film approximately three inches wide by six inches long, it was places over the wrist were it automatically wrapped and fused itself to the skin. Once fused, it matched the texture and color of the user's skin, then it automatically synced with the central computer.

One tap on the wrist would activate a heads up display, which would be projected a few inches above the wrist. This would allow access to most any file in the central data base. Two taps on the wrist would open up communications with immediate team members. Also once the lync was attached, there was no way to remove it. It became a part of the users DNA. Even though severing the arm would get rid of the heads up display, the lync to the central computer would still remain.

Lieutenant Heart, with her newly installed military lync and omega patch on her uniform, headed towards the CSO. As she approached the door, she passed multiple signs in the hallway reading:

"Warning, Restricted Area. No Lyncing allowed beyond this point!"

She reached a closed door with the letters CSO on the outside. She pressed her hand on the scanner and waited. A few minutes after the scan, the top portion of the door opened and the head of the CSO appeared. He noticed the omega patch on her arm and said.

"They really do just give that out to anyone, don't they?"

Inside multiple computers were collating data. Members of the CSO were researching information and manually putting the data in files. Since the CSO was one of the most secure rooms in the military, there was no lyncing allowed inside. Actually, most of the members were only able to use a little under fifteen percent of their mental capacity or were just physically unable to lync at all. This was because this room compiled all data in the five know galaxies. Everything from the number of molecules in any given city to who had the most dangerous weapons and where they were hidden. If someone wanted to take over a planet or even a galaxy, this room would be the key to doing it.

"I'm Lieutenant A. Heart here to pick up a file on last night's incident," she said.

"Well it'll take a few moments to upload it to your lync." The head of the CSO replied.

"Oh." She said.

"I also need a hard copy of that file."

The look on his face turned to disgust for a moment.

"Give someone a little authority and it starts to go to their head." He snickered.

"We're not really set up for that. It will take at least a day to get all that for you. Why don't you come back tomorrow and we'll see what we can do."

He then started to close the door when Lieutenant Heart said, "Not sure if I'm supposed to wait that long. Price said…"

"I don't really care what the councilor said "he interrupted.

"Oh, I guess Commander Johnson will just have to wait then." She said.

And as she was slowly starting to turn away, the door stopped and slowly started to reopen and the room suddenly went quiet. Everyone just stopped and was now looking in Lt. Heart's direction.

"Did you say Commander Johnson?" He asked.

And before she could reply he began speaking in his native tongue. Three people came over to him as he continued speaking. He pointed to a couple different parts of the room while he spoke and then the three CSO members took off running in different directions. Other members soon joined in. The head of the CSO, then turned back to her and said, "Give me fifteen minutes."

Fifteen minutes later he walked over to her with a small folder with all the information she requested along with a flash node. "We printed the information you wanted out in two different font sizes, just in case. We've uploaded the files so you can access them through your lync. This flash node also contains a copy of the files for you, just in case."

Then before he closed the door he said.

"Please tell the Commander that the members of the CSO said thank you."

And as he began to close the door, she could hear the room start to go back to normal. She knew the Commander was well known but she didn't figure that he still garnered this much respect or fear all these years later. But then again he was the co-creator of the DSU and former member of the First Displacers Unit. Not to mention a former member of Recon 15.

She headed down to requisition a vehicle. But she found that Price had already lined one up for her. It was a MHV (military hover vehicle). Though hover vehicles could be used by different level lyncers, only military personnel with a mental level of seventy percent or higher could use a MHV. The thought was that people over seventy percent could not only control all functions of the vehicle but do multiple tasks also without losing control of said vehicle, which would be crucial during a military operation.

As she headed to the commanders location, she began familiarizing herself with the file. The file itself didn't really contain too much information. It said that there was an unknown incident that took place at GF1. A military installation, built on top of the original DSU facility. That it housed only one prisoner and somehow all the defenses had been breached.

Security measured included a gravity fence, security grass and the red grid.

The red grid was an eight foot by eight foot red hot laser grid. Each criss-crossed with smaller three inch by three inch grids that would close on anything that came in contact with it, like a Venus fly trap. It was strong enough to cut through eight feet of the strongest know substance. Not to mention the military personnel stationed there. And if they were to make it through all of that, the biggest obstacle was where the prisoner was kept. It was a room protected by a mental blocking field. Unlike a mental dampening field, a mental blocking field would exert physical pressure on the brain in direct correlation to the amount of mental ability an individual had. So if a person who could use thirty percent of their mental capacity walked into that room, they would experience the physical pressure of thirty percent on their brain. Though the room could be set at a low level it was usually kept at one hundred percent. (It was theorized that a pure lyncer who used eighty five percent or higher would experience a liquefaction of the brain if they entered the room. But of course they could never find a volunteer to test out that theory.

The last obstacle would be the container in which the prisoner was kept. The prisoner's brain had been separated from its body and placed in a special container. Submerged in a highly corrosive organic acid and protected by a multi-level, multi-changing code. If the code is entered incorrectly, the brain is automatically exposed to the acid. And with all of this someone was able to break in. And no information had come out of the facility since. And no one would be allowed in until Commander Johnson arrived on the scene. She wasn't sure why that was or who the prisoner was. But most importantly, what would happen if she couldn't get the Commander to go with her to see the councilor?

Lieutenant Heart was close to the Commander's location when her vehicle slowed to a stop. She looked up and saw a closed fence with what looked like rocks and debris blocking the road ahead. She exited the vehicle and went to see if there was any way around. And as she approached and went to lean on the fence, she almost fell down. It was a hologram but not just any hologram. It was strong enough to fool her vehicle's sensors causing it to stop. She got back in and tried to go forward but the car wouldn't respond. She had to mentally disable the safety features to get the MHV to go through the hologram. About a mile later, someone punched her square in the face. Or at least that's what it felt like as Lieutenant. Heart lost her lync to the vehicle as it nosedived into the ground. Her template (glass sheet used to read files & documents), and the paper files flew all over the vehicle. Once she came to, Lt. Heart slowly exited the vehicle. As she looked back along the dirt road, she saw that her MHV had left a ditch about thirty feet long. She tried to re-lync with the vehicle but she couldn't. She tapped her wrist but her military lync wouldn't connect either. So she gathered up the papers, put them back in the folder and continued up the road. The bright sun beating down on her and the fresh cool air kind of reminded her of home. She then realized that she hadn't heard any sound besides for the wind for awhile. She knew she was far from the city but didn't realize that places like this were so close by. As she came to the end of the road, she was amazed at the site.

There was grass for as far as the eye could see. The sound of water calmly splashing against rocks at the edge of a nearby pond could be heard. But there was nothing else there. Though the file clearly said that Commander Johnson was at this location.

~Was the file wrong? ~ She thought

~Or did he give them the wrong information?~

Just then, off in the distance, she heard someone talking. "Sometimes I wonder about you." The voice said.

As the Lieutenant looked around, she saw a broken white picket fence covered with dark green vines and blood red flowers. Then a large figured appeared from behind it, carrying a folding chair and a cooler.

~It has to be another hologram, ~ she thought,

~because he was too tall to hide behind that small fence.~

The man walked around the fence, set up the chair and slowly sat down, still talking to himself. He opened the cooler and pulled out a drink. Lt. Heart started walking towards him. She noticed that the grass now felt different under her feet. It was making a slight crunching sound with each step, but when she turned around and checked where she had stepped, none of the grass behind her had moved. It was as though no one had even stepped on it.

As she got closer she heard him say.

"What do you mean, I have a guest?"

"Excuse me," She said.

"Commander Johnson?"

He turned around and was kind of surprised. The sun shone brightly off her yellowish skin and golden blonde hair, which seemed to almost hide the slight glow from her reddish eyes. It was a species he hadn't encountered before. And as he looked her over, she looked at him and realized that he kind of looked like Councilor Price.

~They could even be related, ~ she thought to herself.

~Maybe that's how Price knew about…. ~

"Sorry, deliveries go around back." he said.

"What?" She responded.

≈looks like she isn't here to make a delivery.≈ Crystal said to him.

"Then I guess she must be lost then," he said aloud.

"Are you talking to me?" Lieutenant Heart asked.

The Commander looked back towards the fence and said, "Hey! Do you have me out here making her think that I'm talking to myself?"

He then tapped his wrist twice and said.

"Crystal?"

Just then Lt. Heart could hear a female voice laughing.

"Sorry Commander. I saw that her stress levels were a little too elevated while approaching, so I thought this would be a good way to help her out." Crystal said aloud.

"By making her think that I'm crazy?" He asked.

"Well it worked." Crystal said.

"This is Lieutenant Amy Heart, member of the general army. It looks like she has an excellent record. Graduated near the top of her class and even broke a few of your records while training."

"Which records?" the Commander asked.

Ignoring him, Crystal continued.

"She was also the only female, of any species, to graduate from Luccardi's trainings. Not only that but he gave her the highest marks of anyone he's ever trained."

Luccardi and the Commander had been friends a long time and he knew how hard he could be on his trainees so she had to have made some kind of impression during her training.

Turning back to Lieutenant Heart, the Commander asked what she wanted.

Lt. Heart began to speak.

"Councilor Price sent me. He would like you to meet with him in the council chambers regarding a recent incident. Then..."

"Not interested." The Commander interrupted.

"So tell the councilor to find someone else. Besides I'm retired." He added.

"Well I won't bother quoting the Displacers Act to you, since you came up with most of the provisions in it. So you know that in certain cases you can be re-activated," she said.

"Yeah, that's not going to happen. And I really don't appreciate your interrupting me when I'm trying to relax," he said.

"I guess you're afraid. I mean all you had to do was say that you were a coward and I wouldn't have wasted my time here."

Just then, Lt. Heart heard a loud humming sound coming from behind her. As she turned she saw that the security grass, whose tips were glowing bright yellow, were now at eye level. The blades were razor sharp and moving back and forth so fast that it seem to be making the air itself cry, creating that humming noise she was hearing.

"Calm down Crystal, she's entitled to her opinions," the Commander said.

And within a blink of an eye the grass was back to its normal six inch height.

~It had to be security grass, ~ Lt. Heart thought.

~But level three security grass was three inches and only grew to six inches when activated. And though it had a paralyzing neurotoxin, that cause paralysis, it didn't move like that. ~

"Anything else you want to add?" He asked.

"Just that there was an issue at GF1, it was supposedly built on top of the old DSU." She said.

The expression on the Commander's face changed. He then reached out his hand and she handed him the file. As he read through it he got angrier and angrier.

"Bastards!" he said under his breath.

"I should have ended him when I had the chance! Fine, I'll meet with him but we need to make a couple of stops first."

The Commander then said,

"Crystal"

and gave his wrist a tap. The fence rippled and disappeared. A white house, completely surrounded by a white picket fence appeared in its place.

"Dampening field has been deactivated." Crystal said.

"And remember to take my spare node with you. It may come in handy."

The Commander gathered up his things and went into the house. He came out a few minutes later and he and Lt. Heart headed down the road towards her vehicle.

Key-Definitions

Atavus: (at-a-vus) **Classified**

Cycle/Full Cycle: Period of time encompassing a full year. (Approximately 500 days)

Duclos 1, 2 and 3: (do-close) Information relay stations positioned all throughout the universe. Disguised as a dead moon or rock in space hovering just outside the gravitational pull of a black hole.

Lunar Cycle: Period of time from sundown to sunrise. (Approximately 17 hours)

Full Lunar Cycle: Period of time from sundown to sundown. (Approximately 30 hours)

Solar Cycle: Period of time from sunrise to sundown. (Approximately 13 hours)

Full Solar Cycle: Period of time from sunrise to sunrise. (Approximately 30 hours) **Note**: (10 Solar/Lunar Cycles equal 1 week)

Recon Teams/Units: Five man teams used to search the universe for any signs of Displacer activities. **Note**: (Most of these would become the foundation for the DSU)

Tholian: (tho-lee-an) From the coldest and most mountainous region of the planet Olin. They stand 7' to 9' tall. Their face and hands are humanoid...ish. Their feet have long claws which enable them to grab and climb. With emerald green eyes and a soft white fur, covering the rest of their body. **Note**: (When they sense danger their eyes turn black and their fur changes to a hard metal like substance, giving it a blueish grey color.)

Veagans: (vay-gans) Race of mercenaries with shape shifting abilities. Specializing in infiltration, espionage and assassination.

Tholian Warriors: Tholians who voluntarily go through a process called "De-Evolution" This process of genetic manipulation causes their entire body to be covered in fur which while white in appearance is actually a harder metal than what their fur changes to when they sense danger. Their eyes, which can barely be seen through the fur covering their face, turn dark red. Their teeth become razor sharp and their mental state becomes just one step above that of a savage beast. **Note**: (to counter this they are imprinted with an overwhelming urge to protect their pack or tribe at all costs)

Zenobian: (zee-no-bee-an) Merchant traders, their dark skin and freakishly long hair, 3'-4', make them easily recognizable. Their ability to sell or trade anything coupled with their quick wit and even temperedness has made them the go to race for all manners of negotiations.

Zenobian Warriors: Every few generations a handful of Zenobians are born with a chameleon like camouflage ability and really really short tempers. Once these traits emerge they are immediately taken from their families and placed into warrior training.

Chapter III

In Mrs. Smith's classroom on of her students began speaking.

"In most cultures and or societies, there is usually a varying set of beliefs about how their culture began. But ours is a little different. Because all of our societies shared the same ending it eventually gave way to our mutual re-birth. One hundred and fifty totally different species and life forms melded together to create something unique. A brand new society, that has taken the best of each and created a new way of being. But there is always the threat that they will return. The ones responsible for our societies ending. The ones ultimately responsible for our new beginning. The ones we referred to as....The Displacers.

As Lt. Heart and the Commander headed towards town, she couldn't help but notice all the scars on his arms and legs. While he was re-reading the report, she could see that though his skin, like councilor Price's, was not that dark, the scars that he had were.

"So you must be a pure lyncer in order to work at the core." Mrs. Smith said. "A pure lyncer then compress their memories and place it into a zip file so that they can utilize the full potential of their eighty five percent or more mental capacity."

Just then the door opened slightly but no one was there.

"Ok?" Mrs. Keller said.

"Who did that?"

But the class remained silent. As she turned back to the class a face appeared at the door then quickly disappeared. The students began to chuckle as Mrs. Smith looked back to see an empty doorway. They could tell that she wasn't amused as she looked back at them. Just then the Commander walked in.

"Hey Sis, How's it going?" he asked.

She just threw him a look. A small murmur began to come over her students.

"Now settle down class." She said,

"Looks like we have an unexpected guest. And how do we great guests?" She asked.

The whole class turned towards the door and in unison said.

"Good Morning!"

"Nice." He responded.

"Looks like you have them trained well." He said with a smile.

"Excuse me." A student, whose desk lit up said,

"Are you him? The First Displacers team captain?"

"Guess my reputation precedes me, even here." he said.

"Yes, that's correct. Though it's former."

"I knew it!" he exclaimed.

"I knew it! You're Commander Johnson. So does that mean that Mrs. Smith was a former member of your unit also?"

"Are you happy now?" She said.

"Always causing trouble everywhere you go."

"Yeah, I know. Sorry about that." He said.

    Then he turned to the class and said.

"Well you know that according to the Displacers act, even if she was a part of my unit, only Mrs. Smith is allowed to disclose that information. " Adding,

"The Displacers Act has that very important rule and it has helped to keep our society safe for many years now."

"Class," Mrs. Smith interrupted,

"check digital files fifteen and sixteen about the five percent rule. I will return momentarily." She said as she walked out the door with the Commander close behind.

Once in the hallway, she gave him a big hug.

"You know, you could stop by more often to say hi." She scolded.

"Besides the girls like when you come to visit."

"Yeah, yeah but you know that I don't like to intrude. So how are the little ones doing?" He asked.

"They're good." She said.

"And Mike." He asked.

"He's doing good also." She replied asking,

"So what brings you by?"

"Well I just wanted to check in with you. That's all." He said.

But the look she gave him told him that she didn't believe that.

"TROY!" She said intently.

"What?" He said giving her that innocent look.

"Don't worry sis. If it was something really bad, I'd let you know."

"So the military escort is just for???" She asked looking beyond him and down the hallway.

"Oh, you mean the rookie?" The Commander said smiling.

"Well you know how Price can be."

"Well don't go getting into any trouble." She said as she headed back to the classroom.

She knew something must be up, especially if he stopped in just to visit her and here of all places. As she walked back into the classroom, she noticed that the discussion had turned slightly hostile towards one student.

"What's going on here?" She asked loudly.

"Why are you not checking the files like I asked?"

A students desk lights up and he spoke.

"Well, Mrs. Smith, she says that her planet was saved by the Commander but we learned that he retired twenty years ago, so she's not telling the truth."

"But it's the truth," a small female student stated.

"He did save our planet along with the rest of DSU-1.

Specialist Keller and Lt….." But she was interrupted by another student.

"You heard the Commander, the Displacers Act is supposed to keep the names of its members a secret."

"Now hold on class." Mrs. Smith interrupted.

"She just arrived and hasn't learned all of our rules yet, that's why she's in our class." Mrs. Smith stated.

"Ok, are you sure about the Commander saving your planet. He did retire sometime ago." She asked.

"Yes," the student replied.

"Our planet did not have the same kind of deep space propulsion system as a lot of others. So we had to be placed in cryo-pods for our journey here and during that time, our entire planets history, up until the very last day, was fed into our pods while we slept."

"So what planet are you from then?" She asked.

"Meagan 3," The girl responded.

20 cycles ago

"Commander? Did you just use a Plasma Grenade?" Specialist Keller asked.

"Ummmm no...No I didn't. But I think Kent might have." The Commander responded.

"Ok. What's going on?" She asked.

"Sorry but I'm declaring a Category Three Omega Level threat. So tell the Meagans that they have about thirty minutes to evacuate the planet." He said.

The Chancellor began yelling about them not having authority to do that.

"Sis, can you deal with that?" He asked.

"I'm sure the Veagans have made landfall by now, so stay in the command center. We'll signal you when we arrive."

"Ok, understood." She said.

"Be safe."

"Always." The Commander responded.

She then turned to deal with the Chancellor.

"Sir, please calm down. Now if you'd take out your contract I can explain why this is happening."

The Chancellor pulled out a crystal tablet and pulled up the file. Nicki tapped her wrist once and scrolled up until she found their contract. As she began speaking a thirty minute timer popped up on her lync and began counting down. It also appeared on both the Chancellor's contract and the contract on her heads up display.

"Now this is our standard contract, that you signed and as you'll remember, we went over the entire contact before you signed it. But here again, in the first section, it clearly states that while this contract is in effect that you will be placed under the Pelham Accord until the contract has been filled. And if an Omega Level threat occurs and is confirmed by two or more members of the DS Unit assigned to this contract, then you agree to follow the rules of the accord as stated."

"Well then I want to cancel this contract." The Chancellor exclaimed.

"Well that's fine." She responded.

"You can cancel the contract at anytime but just know that once the protocol has been enacted, no one can cancel it. And as you can see by the timer, you now have twenty seven minutes left to evacuate." She then added,

"Oh, and threatening me or trying to shoot down the Commander's ship will not change anything. Most likely it'll just make him mad. He'll enact the protocol no matter what you do. Also, if you were fortunate enough to stop him, this signal has been sent out and at least five other Displacer units who are already on their way here. They'll make sure that the protocol was enacted, shoot down any ship trying to flee the planet and ask questions later."

Now while the chancellor and his general were discussing their options, one of the officers sent out the evacuation signal. The Chancellor was definitely not happy as he then began yelling,

"Who sent that signal? I didn't give that order!"

And though she had seen who did it, she just smiled and said,

"Well now that that's settled I'll be waiting up on the roof for my ride."

Once on the ship, Nicki headed for the bridge. She could see the Commander but not Lt. Kent. As she sat down she asked.

"What happened out there? One minute you were just checking the perimeters then the next thing I know you're…wait? What's that smell?" She asked.

As she looked around the bridge, she could see the Commander's plasma rifle leaning against his chair.

"You know," She said,

"Since I've been a part of your unit, I've only asked a few things, the last one being that if you're in a fire fight, to please not leave your weapons up here. You know that smell really bothers me. Why don't you have Kent clean it? He's not usually that busy. By the way, where is Kent?"

"The Lt. Is…." Crystal started to say before the Commander interrupted.

"He didn't make it."

"But he was just…." Nicki began to say.

"He didn't make it," The Commander repeated as he quickly stood up. Grabbing his plasma rifle, he slowly headed towards the hatchway. He dropped Crystal's node in Nicki's hand as he passed her and said.

"Can you look this over and let me know if you come to the same conclusion as I did?"

"What conclusion is that?" She asked.

But the Commander just ignored her and walked out the hatchway. She started to ask Crystal what had happened to Kent but as she did the Commander stopped and said.

"Crystal, let me know when we're in range to enact the first stage of the NGZ-301."

He then continued walking adding.

"Some of those files might be a bit graphic."

Then the Commander headed towards the armory.

Nicki plugged the node into the console in front of her and began scanning through the files. She clicked onto the first file and began watching it. It seemed to be a normal documentation of a scientific experiment, and then it got really graphic really fast. If this was any indication of what was going on down there then it's no wonder why the Veagans brought a battle cruiser to that planet. She barely made it through the video and wasn't sure if she would be able to handle the rest. But after watching the first one, she scanned through the file names and one caught her eye. She wasn't sure why but the numbers attached to one of the files just seemed familiar so she clicked on it and started watching.

~Is that? ~ She thought to herself.

Then as she watched more, she realized who was on the vid and why the numbers seemed so familiar. It was the date of her wedding, and the ones on the screen were DSU-1 minus her. It was the mission that the Commander had to leave her wedding for and the one who took her place was...Just then the vid cut off.

"Crystal, what happened? And was that?" Nicki asked.

"Not sure what you mean." Crystal replied.

"Why did the vid cut off?" Nicki asked.

"You are not authorized to see classified material."

"How is that classified?" she asked adding,

"The Commander just gave that to me. So you can't classify it."

"Actually it wasn't me who did. You know that our systems are directly connected to the central computers, so classifying a file can be instituted instantaneously on their end." Crystal explained, adding.

"I guess you'll have to ask the Commander about the rest of the vid."

The Commander, sitting in the armory, was cleaning his weapon when Nicki walked in.

"Yes, you were right." She said.

The Commander didn't respond, he just kept cleaning his weapon.

"Did you look through all the videos?" she asked.

Again, he didn't answer.

"I just wanted to ask about the video labeled atvs-2-9-02…..

TROY?" she shouted.

Then Crystal chimed in,

"Commander, we're in range of stage one."

"How many ships have evacuated?" He asked.

"About thirty percent but there's still about seventeen minutes before the deadline. "She replied.

"Fire stage one, then head to the next coordinates to fire stage two. Also send a message to the Veagan battle cruiser. Let them know that we will be initiating a level three quarantine on this entire planet within fifteen minutes. "He said.

"Why would you inform them?" Nicki asked.

"Well we know why they're here and by letting them know that we're about to remedy the situation while also giving them a chance to get away. Means that maybe they would owe us one." He answered.

"Yes, if they acknowledge our signal," Crystal said.

But she did as he said and as the ship sped off towards the upper atmosphere, a missile was launched towards the surface. It headed towards the largest body of water, which would take about fifteen minutes to reach, where it would then burrow its way to the planets core.

The NGZ-301 was one of three weapons used for a permanent planetary quarantine. Negative Zero to the three hundredth and first power-grenade was what most liked to call it. Simply put: it was a two-staged system that could turn any planet into a giant snow globe, then into a giant ball of ice. The first part would seek out the largest body of water where it would burrow into the planet's core. The chemicals on the outside of the missile would be removed and react to the water. Once the missile reached the planets core the resulting chemical reaction would not only freeze the core solid but would continue to freeze everything up to the surface. The second part would be launched from the upper stratosphere, where the chemicals would spread out over the entire planet. Once saturated, the chemicals would bond causing a thin layer of ice to cover the troposphere, which would start to hinder sunlight from entering. Then a loud "Crunch!" would be heard by anyone left on the planet's surface as a one mile thick layer of ice would appear beneath the troposphere, causing a vacuum like effect as the air pressure changed. Then over and over again, as mile after mile of ice would appear until the ice from above met with the planet's surface, forming a perfectly sealed ball of planetary ice.

It was clear that the Commander was not going to discuss the issue any further with specialist Keller, so she headed back to the bridge.

A while later Crystal launched stage two just as the Commander walked onto the bridge. She explained that about eighty seven percent of the population had successfully been evacuated but that the Veagan ship was still on the surface.

"Well once the quarantine is complete, we'll wrap a stasis field around the planet and move it to the furthest orbit from the sun." The Commander stated.

"That'll cause a temporary ice age on her sister planet." Crystal informed him.

"Yes but they are only animals and vegetation so, no worries." He responded.

Just then Crystal detected a signal.

"Commander, looks like the Veagan ship is taking off."

"Well nothing we can do about that, we gave them fair warning." He replied.

The first mile of ice had appeared and the second was just about to appear when Crystal said'

"The signal is getting closer."

They all began watching the planet when a large blur began to appear within the ice. Then after a minute or so a ship emerged from the ice but it didn't break or disturb the ice in anyway. It was just there.

"Did they just phase through the ice?" The Commander asked.
"They actually have phase technology!" He said excitedly.
"Commander I'm getting a signal. It's some kind of code
followed by one word." Crystal said.
"Well?" He said.
"What's the word?"
"Loosely translated it says "gratitude". But I'm not sure what
the code is."
"Isn't it obvious? They owe us one, so it's a call me if you need
me signal, "He said with a smile. "Now let's lasso this puppy
up and put it in its new home. "

Once the process was finished they wrapped a stasis field
around the planet, ripped it from its orbit and placed it so that it
was in the furthest orbit around the sun. The Commander then
had Nicki send a message to Councilor Price informing him
that we'll meet him in the council chambers and to please have
Dr. Z there as well. As the ship sped off, each member of the
crew thought about what had happened during this mission and
the videos that each of them saw.

The Commander, now sitting in his quarters, was just
staring at his weapon and as the ship began to speed off into
the darkness of space, a song could be heard playing
throughout their ship.

¥ I can't believe you left me in the end

And all this time I thought that we were friends

Why don't you just let things be

Hoping you will forget me

Hoping you will…..forget

Hoping you will…..forget

Hoping you will…..forget

Hoping you will…..forget me. ¥

As Commander Johnson walked out of the learning center, he stopped, closed his eyes, took a breath and slowly exhaled. "Ok, I'm ready. He said.

"Ok, so you're ready to go see Councilor Price now?" Lt. Heart asked.

"No," he replied.

"I figure we should head over to GF1 first, and then go see the councilor afterwards."

She tried to object but using his thumb, the Commander pointed over his shoulder and said

"Well it's just over that hill, so it just makes sense to go check it out now," He said with a smile.

Vehicles and military personnel had formed a perimeter just outside the gravity fence when the commander and the Lt. drove up. They were directed to Captain Beckett, who had been in charge of the facility for the past few years. He had been ordered not to re-enter the facility until the consultant had arrived, which did not sit well with him. He was standing on the back of his vehicle, which was parked on the grass, next to the driveway leading to the facility.

"Are you the consultant we've been waiting for?" Captain Beckett asked.

"Well we were…" Lt. Heart said.

But the Commander interrupted.

"Yes, yes I am." He said as he began walking on the grass towards the gravity fence.

"Commander!" She shouted.

He stopped and looked back at her.

"That's a gravity fence you're about to walk into."

"Really?" He said as he began to put his hand up to it.

"Yes, you know the kind that can mimic any planet's gravity times a hundred. If you approach it at the wrong speed you can be instantly crushed or repelled back so fast that it could break every bone in your body."

"Really?" He repeated as he put his hand through the fence.

"Well would you look at that." He said.

"Nothing happened."

She looked at the captain and asked if he had deactivated the fence.

"No", he replied,

"we were told to wait outside the fence until you arrived so we haven't done anything but take a few readings."

Commander Johnson then said,

"Oh, I just figured if everyone had disappeared then the fence probably did also."

But as she looked above his head, she could still see the warning signs moving along the gravity fence, so she didn't know what to think. The Commander then headed towards the driveway, stopped and said with a smile,

"Well, after you captain." The Commander said.

The Captain tapped his lync and instructed his men to move in and search the area. Medical was to stand by outside the perimeter. Commander Johnson, LT. Heart, Captain Beckett and a couple of his men entered the main facility.

For the most part it was empty. There were a few monitors high up on the walls. A couple of terminals, one near the entrance and on the far wall near a dark doorway.

"Not much here, huh?" The Commander asked adding,

"Guess you guys are still in the middle of redecorating the place."

"This place was built for only one reason. And that was to hold the most dangerous members of society. Of course we only had one occupant since the facility opened." Captain Beckett said.

"Had," The Commander emphasized.

"Well we haven't confirmed that yet. This place has the most state-of-the-art security imaginable. Outside we have the gravity fence, security grass and the red grid. Inside we have 'The Room'. It's equipped with a mental blocking field. Unlike the mental dampening field, this not only blocks mental lyncing but it applies mental pressure equal to the amount of mental ability one has. So if your MLP is thirty percent then thirty percent of physical pressure would be applied to your brain." Captain Beckett said.

"It's speculated that if you have a MLP of eighty five percent or higher, that your brain would be liquefied, turned into a black ooze. But we've never gotten anyone with that high of a MLP to actually test that out for us."

As they walked through what looked to be an empty facility the commander began to feel a little light headed. They headed for the only visible doorway, which was against the right hand wall. Captain Beckett entered a code on the panel then placed his hand on it. The door slowly opened revealing a darkened room. It had grey floors, black walls, some kind of mist or fog blocking the view of the ceiling but a light red glow could be seen emanating from it. Sitting In the center of the room was a medium sized cylinder.

"Are you sure it's safe to enter?" Lt. Heart asked.

"Yes, it should be. The mental blocking field is controlled by the CSO and they informed me that the field had been deactivated." Captain Beckett replied.

"That cylinder has two separate sections. One which contains the brain of the prisoner and the other is filled with an organic acid. There is a multi-changing sixteen digit code which rotates every five minutes and if the wrong code is entered, even once, then the acid would be released destroying the brain."

Just then the Commander went down to one knee.

"You ok?" Lt. Heart asked.

"Yeah, I just got a bit light headed." He said.

Of course the pain he actually felt made him miss the warning Crystal had issued.

Lt. Heart excitedly said,

"Your nose!"

And as the Commander put his hand up to wipe his nose, he realized that there was blood on it and it was black. The Captain was shocked, since the CSO had assured him that the dampening field was off but it was more shocking for Captain Beckett who was wondering why the Commander was the only one affected.

Lt. Heart had a different thought.

~If it only happens to people over eighty five percent, then why was he being affected? According to councilor Price and the

commanders file, he was only supposed to be at around thirty
five percent~

"I'll be ok." He said.

"I just need to go outside for a bit."

As he continued wiping the rest of the blood way from his
nose, he noticed that a message was flashing across his wrist.
His wrist was flashing red with the words "Code Black!"
scrolling across it in black letters.

"Captain, we need to evacuate the facility." The Commander
said.

"What? Why? Just because you're not feeling well doesn't
mean that we need to suspend our investigation. We need to
ascertain what happened here."

The Commander held his wrist up for Captain Beckett to
see.

Captain Beckett said, "Code Black? There's no such thing
and I will not…"

But Lt. Heart interrupted him.

"Sir, do you know what's underneath this building? It's the
original DSU facility. Now I don't know what they have stored
down there but I can only imagine that the Commander does.
So if he says we need to evacuate this place, then we should
probably listen to him."

"Commander, I'm detecting a distortion field and it's getting stronger." Crystal said.

Slowly rising to his feet. The Commander shouted. "Captain! We need to evacuate now!" He then said, "Crystal!"

A female voice came from the lync on his wrist saying "Understood."

Crystal tapped into the facilities communication system and her voice echoed throughout the facility. "Warning! Synge {singe} protocol is in effect. Please evacuate the facility immediately. I repeat, Synge protocol is in effect. Please evacuate the facility immediately!"

Multiple voices began coming out of the captain's lync. Captain Beckett tapped his wrist twice and said, "This is Captain Beckett. There is a potential Omega level threat. Evacuate the facility as quickly as possible." "Have your men gather about 100 yards outside the gravity fence. Also make sure they don't remove anything from the facility. They need to leave it just the way they found it." The Commander said.

The Captain didn't like being told what to do, especially by him but he reluctantly obliged. "All personnel, rendezvous point is one hundred yards outside of the gravity fence. Also take only what you brought in. Do not, I repeat; do not take anything out of the facility." Captain Beckett said into his lync.

Outside the sound of military boots could be heard quickly moving away from the facility. Inside the facility it was relatively quiet as the three of them made their way back to the door when they heard a loud thud. And as the Captain and Lt. Heart looked back they saw the Commander was face down on the floor. She rushed over to see if he was ok. "Commander!" She shouted.

As she bent down to check him, she motioned to Captain Beckett to help her. She then ran outside to grab a portable hover bed from one of the medical personnel before they got beyond the gate. Then as the two of them helped the Commander onto it Crystal's voice became garbled as it was piped through the communication system.

"Tem…poral…..dis..pla..ment…….em..i…nent."

"What did she just say?" Captain. Beckett asked.

"I don't know," replied Lt. Heart. "But I think that we need to get out of here as soon as possible."

As they pushed the Commander out of the facility, they could see that the sky around the facility had changed. Though it was still daytime, the area above and immediately outside the facility was dark. The Captain and Lieutenant were able to get the Commander outside of the gravity fence just in time. As they turned back to look the sky right above the facility had turned black, clouds were swirling around above the building and the wind began to intensify. Then suddenly it stopped. The air was calm. The clouds above the building became stationary and it became eerily quiet.

"What just happened?" Captain Beckett asked.

And before Lt. Heart could answer a voice said.

"It's not over yet."

The two of them looked back to see that the Commander had gotten up and was attempting to get off the hover bed.

"You need to stay put until we have someone look at you." The Lieutenant said.

"No, I'm better now. I just needed some air." The Commander responded.

Just then there was quick flash of light.

"Was that?" Lt Heart asked.

"No, couldn't be." Captain Beckett said.

Then there was another flash.

"That can't really be happening can it? I mean the pure lyncers at the core have never done that before." Captain Beckett said.

"No, it's not what you think," the Commander said.

Before Capt. Beckett could respond, there was a blinding light and after a few seconds, the sound of gun fire soon followed.

"Firing! Who's firing?" The Captain yelled.

But the sounds were coming from the other side of the gravity fence, not from his men. Then the sound of vehicles could be heard driving around, then silence. The light faded and vehicles could now be seen on the other side of the gravity fence, though none were there when they arrived. The area around the facility was still dark like it was night time on one side of the fence and daytime on the other. Through the silence, the sound of military boots could be heard echoing all around them.

"This makes no sense. What's going on over there?" Captain Beckett yelled into his lync.

Screams then echoed through the darkness and then a dull thud could be heard. And as they all looked on a body appeared on the ground, then another and another. Bodies began appearing all over the area around the facility. Some against the walls, some on top of the vehicles, a few even appeared in mid air before drooping to the ground with a soft thud. They didn't appear all at once or in rapid succession but at a slow and steady pace before suddenly stopping. And not one of them appeared outside of the gravity fence.

"We need to get medical in there right away," Captain Beckett said as he started to tap his wrist.

"No, hold on." The Commander warned.

"They could still be alive." He said ignoring the Commander.

Captain Beckett then tapped his wrist twice and said. "All medical personnel…"

The Commander interrupted.

" It's a TDG."

"What's a TDG?" Lt. Heart asked.

Then the sound of soft rain could be heard. Puzzled, the Captain and the Lieutenant looked around for the source and after a few moments they noticed that a few small red puddles had begun forming in the grass.

Key-Definitions

The Council: 13 members of society picked to write and enforce laws. They deal with all disputes and court cases, not that there are many of the latter. Once the original 12 members start to retire their replacements will be picked from the populace by vote and will serve a term no longer than five cycles. **Note**: (At this time there are only 12 council members. The 13th originally refused the position but said he could be called upon if there is ever a tie vote between the other 12 members)

Decontamination Procedure: Procedure in which anyone new to the planet or who has been off world for more than 7 full solar/lunar cycles has to go through. This process determines if you have any Displacers or Veagan cells within your body. **Note**: (Anyone with a Physical Lync can bypass this because their Lync allows the central computer to monitor their vitals at all times)

Meagan 3: The only known duel planetary orbit to exist in the entire universe. These two planets are so close together that they are caught in each other's gravitational pull and the only thing keeping them from colliding and ripping each other apart is the fact that a small satellite/moon is caught directly in between them.

Lyncers: (link-ers) Anyone with the ability to link their mind to other people, machines or weapons.

Non-Lyncers: Those who do not have the ability to lync. **Note**: (Usually those with a MLP of 19% or less.)

Orientation and interplanetary Education: Facility where anyone new to the planet is sent, after quarantine, to be educated with all of our laws and lifeforms. **Note**: (This Facility is equipped to handle and support all lifeforms. The underground sections of the facility even contain, dark sections where no light exists, gaseous sections as well as sections submerged with water and filled with lava just to name a few)

Physical Lync: Biometric device that fuses with ones DNA to create a physical link between the user and the central computer. It monitors and records everything from what the team members sees to their vital signs. **Note**: (This can also be used to connect with other team members who aren't mentally connected as well as pulling up a heads up display that can allow the user to access any file in the central computer)

Pure Lyncers: Anyone with a MLP of 85% or above.

Valerians: (va-lair-ians) A species that's born with a thick green like reptilian skin. As they grow older a humanoid like skin grows over it. **Note**: (The female of the species are born with jet black hair which can grow down to their shoulders or to the middle of their back)

Chapter IV

A backup server kicked in at the Central Security Office, then a second one.

"What's going on?" Raney {rainy}, the head of the CSO asked.

"The system finally connected with GF1 and so much information is flooding in that it's trying to over load the system," Someone yelled out.

At that point a third server kicked in making Raney nervous. Backup servers were there in case the main system went down and that has never happened, so they've never really been used. And for three servers to be activated, especially when there's no issue with the main server, is troubling to say the least.

Back at the learning center a student is speaking.

"Our sun is actually a Synge, what some cultures call a celestial dragon. They're born from eggs that are laid in stars. They take more than a millennia to hatch. Most stars burn out before they do which is why there are so few in existence. They float through space consuming all manner of debris. Though once they consume a certain amount of organic material their skin produces a liquid which when exposed to the vacuum of space ignites. They are not tame and cannot be domesticated but with the mental powers that we have at our disposal, we are able to keep it here for our needs. And since we feed it a steady diet, it seems to be content here as well."

Nicki wandered towards the window while the child continued to speak when suddenly she felt a sharp pain in her side which almost made her double over. And though she hadn't lynced with Crystal or the Commander in years, she knew that something was terribly wrong.

~I hope everything's ok over there.~ She thought.

~Huh, who would have guessed that the end of the world would lead to this? ~

Nicki awoke to the smell of fresh coffee brewing. As she slowly opened her eyes, she noticed that Mike had already gotten up. She made her way to the kitchen and found Mike cooking breakfast. He handed her a cup of coffee and said "Good morning."

She took it and smiled. The global news was on talking about some kind of anomaly heading towards the planet and as Mike and Nicki began making small talk a loud siren sounded. The people on the news looked startled. The global newsfeed turned bright red and flashed three times. The siren sounded again and the screen flashed three more times.

"This just in, the anomaly has entered our upper atmosphere and is rapidly heading towards B-City."

"This has got to be some kind of joke," Mike said.

But before he could continue Nicki's phone went off. The message read "Please head to your designated evacuation center. This is not a drill! Mandatory planetary evacuation is in effect!"

Mike then received a message on his phone.

"Guess this isn't a joke. This says that I have to report to the mine."

"Why?" She asked.

"You need to head to the evacuation center."

"Sorry but I have to make sure that the mine is secure and that the crystals are loaded and shipped off planet," he replied.

Mike had worked in the mine for years. His job was to inspect the crystals for their purity. Theirs was the only planet in the system that produced the crystals and they were used for everything from lasers to tablets and were the planets most valuable export.

"We both have an important job to do and as the one who will mold the minds of our future generations, your safety is definitely a priority. Besides your children will probably be scared and need all their instructors there to help keep them calm." Mike said.

"But." Nicki said before Mike interrupted her.

"I'll be ok. I'll make sure everything is secure on my end, then I'll evacuate as well."

"Ok but I'm going to keep the ship on the platform until you arrive." Nicki said.

"I'm sure we'll have our own shuttle for...." Mike said but Nicki interrupted.

"I said, we'll be waiting on the platform until you arrive." Mike knew he wouldn't win that argument so he just smiled and said, "ok". They both got ready and then headed out to their separate destination.

On the outer edge of the galaxy, Recon 15 was on routine patrol.

"Looks like we have a disturbance near the central planet of this system," Troy said.

"Probably just another false alarm," Pat replied.

"Well we still have to check it out," Devon said.

They began to change course and headed towards the planet.

Recon teams were made of five members and patrolled the three known galaxies for possible Displacer activities. Their job was not to engage the enemy but to report any activity they encounter.

Back on the planet surface, Nicki had arrived at the ship and began a head count. The children were nervous; they had been through a couple of drills before but this time it was real. Not only were they on a ship that was being prepped for launch but some had actually witnessed the fear in their parent's eyes. They were children growing up in a world that had never really encountered war: civil or otherwise. Yes, there had been accidents before, and yes, people had died. But not like this. Not on a global scale. Their planet was being seized by an unknown alien force and most couldn't comprehend why. They were taught that their planet was the only one in the system that produced the Norah Crystal, a key component in most lasers and the main one needed for most hyper-drive and sub-light engines. But they would have been shocked if they knew the real reason for this invasion.

Nicki finished her count and began to conference with the instructors on the other transports. It was pretty chaotic at first which made some of the children start to cry. Reports were coming in of strange glimmering lights falling from the sky and people being attacked and killed. There was a slight muffled explosion right before she lost contact with one of the instructors. She wasn't sure what had happened but suddenly found that none of her communication devices were working either. She had no way of contacting Mike or knowing where he was. At that point the automatic countdown began as ships across the planet began to lift off. Nicki yelled at the pilot to stop the countdown because they needed to wait for Mike. Of course her yelling frightened the kids even more so she had to stop, compose herself, and then calm them down once again. She moved to the hatch and looked out to see if Mike was near. Their launch site was actually near her house and the instructional facility where she taught. It was on the beach and had a seaside view. She always did love the view there. Out of the corner of her eye she noticed something shiny. As she turned to look she saw something in the sky slowly floating down towards them. It almost looked like a humanoid body but with multiple arms. Then she noticed that it wasn't just one of them but that the sky was full of them, like a hundred giant crystal snowflakes. It was kind of beautiful she thought until she realized that these were probably the aliens that were invading her planet. Just then one of the crystal figures shattered. Then another, soon she realized that there was gun fire coming from further down the beach. Four dark figures in strange uniforms were running down the beach shooting at the alien invaders. Suddenly a face appeared from her left and Nicki jumped back. A dark face stared at her, smiled and said "Hey, how's it going?"

She was so shocked that she couldn't even speak.

"Sorry didn't mean to scare you but I really think you guys should go." He said.

Nicki eventually snapped out of it and said,

"We can't. Mike isn't here yet, and we can't leave without him."

"Sorry to hear that but you really should go," he replied. "We're not even supposed to be down here. Our job is to observe and report. The only reason we intervened was because you guys wouldn't have been able to launch if we didn't. Your whole planet is being overrun and we won't be able to hold them off for much longer."

As they talked, the rest of Recon 15 was clearing a path above their ship for a clear trajectory.

"Troy!" A voice rang out from down the beach.

"I told you about getting friendly with the natives! Let's get a move on. We can't stay long."

He turned back towards Nicki and said,

"Sorry, gotta go and so do you."

Just as he was about to run off he turned back and shouted.

"If you guys don't have a place to meet up or a rallying point. Then head behind the fourth planet. We have a temporary mobile base for re-supplying and for the injured."

He then took off down the beach, joined the others and began firing above the ship as well. She watched more crystalline figures shattering above as the hatch suddenly close and the engines began to fire. Nicki turned and headed towards the pilot.

"What are you doing?" She yelled "We need to wait for…"

But the pilot interrupted.

"We're leaving! Didn't you hear what that guy said? If we wait any longer we might not make it at all. Besides, aren't you in charge of their future?" He said, looking back towards the children.

She looked out at the frightened faces behind her knowing that he was right.

"Strap in!" He shouted,

"This might get rough."

As the ship began to lift off, Nicki realized that they did not have a preset destination. Yes, they had an evacuation plan in case of a planetary emergency but it was just to escape impending disaster. Across the planet there were only a dozen of these ships, not counting privately owned ones. And though they would try to save the children, the planet's history, the Norah Crystals, and those key to their survival, they didn't have another planet to go to.

The shooting on the beach had stopped as Recon 15 watched the ship lift off.

"Guess it's time we joined them." Devon said.

Outside the planet ships were scattering away heading in all different directions.

As a few ships headed behind the fourth planet a large object came into view. It wasn't just one object but a bunch of smaller ones joined together to create a larger one. Each had its own unique shape and markings. They formed what appeared to be a giant sphere with a string of ships on different sides, like a giant flail.

Inside there was some gravity and the air felt stale. And though it did resemble a sphere on the outside, the inside was sectioned off by the walls from each ship forming a sort of maze. A few ships from the planet docked to seek medical attention and to figure out where they should go. Though Nicki tried to concentrate on the meeting, her thoughts could only focus on where Mike was and how she could find him.

Once the meeting ended she found herself wandering around the station. There were strange markings along the walls which of course she didn't recognize but she followed them none the less and then happened upon a bar. Inside there was a strange looking fellow behind a makeshift bar. He was about her height but chubby with long, black scraggly hair. "A bar? Here?" She asked.

"Of course," The man replied.

"When people watch their planet get invaded by an alien species or destroyed, they usually need a good drink," he said smiling.

Nicki could actually agree with that because she needed a drink right about now herself. There were only a few people in the bar besides Nicki and the bartender. Some were civilians but most were members of other recon units and though she hadn't seen a lot of this makeshift station or the infirmary. To her the bar seemed fairly large.

Across the room there were people seated at a table gambling. On the other side of them, seated at tables along the wall, were members of Recon 15. Nicki didn't recognize them until the one with the shaved head walked in and headed towards the table where the gambling was going on. "Who's that?" Nicki asked the bartender.

Looking up and across the room he answered. "Who? The loud one that just came in? Oh that's Troy a member of Recon 15. But if you meet him he'll probably ask you to call him Commander. Yeah that Johnson is a strange one. The rest of his team is here as well. The one directly across from us is Devon but most people call him Price. The buff one with the Afro polishing that big weapon at the table behind him is Patrick, Pat for short. The thinner one sitting next to him is Alexander but he likes being called AJ. And the older gentleman at the table in the back is Moe but they all call him Granddad."

Troy had ventured up to one of the players at the table. "So is this her?" He asked looking back at AJ. "Yeah," Jay responded, "that's JP."

Troy looked her up and down but she paid him no mind. "Who's he staring at over there?" Nicki asked.

"Oh well that's trouble, even more so than Johnson. They call her JP and she's a member of the Wild Bunch. A group of mercenaries that will do anything if the price is right. From assassinations to kidnapping to toppling governments. I'm surprised to see her this far out. Some say she's some kind of hybrid but doubt you'd want to ask her what she's a hybrid of. Though I heard her called a Valerian. "

"A Valerian? What's a Valerian?" Nicki asked.

"Shhh. Keep your voice down," he said slowly looking her way. "You don't want to offend her. Actually I've never seen a Valerian. I've heard that they have lizard like skin and…."

But he froze in his tracks when he saw her look away from her cards and in his general direction.

Troy stood hovering on JP's left hand side while she was still staring at the bartender and Nicki before looking back down at her cards.

"Can I help you?" She asked, never once looking up.

She wasn't very tall. Maybe around 5'6" or so. She had shoulder length black hair. Her eyes were a light brown almost hazel. Her skin, cream color but depending on the light it could be considered white or even mocha. She had a short sleeved camouflage shirt on and a pair of camouflage shorts as well.

"No, I'm just admiring the beauty," Troy said with a smile.

"Look at those curves. I mean come on guys; I can't be the only one drooling over her here. Who would believe that we'd find an LPR, here of all places? I mean that is a Luna-Sol Light-Particle Rifle, correct?"

Referring to the rifle strapped across her back.

"One of those weapons, constructed by an ancient civilization, that was able to utilize light as a weapon. Or in this case an actual projectile. The technology it must have taken to create something so beautiful. To take an actual beam of sunlight, cut it into small pieces and use each piece as a projectile creating the ultimate sniper rifle. A projectile that not only travels at the speed of light but leaves no trace. That has got to be one of the rarest weapons in the universe."

He then slowly reached out his hand to touch it.

JP had not moved during his little monologue. She had her cards in her right hand, grabbed her drink with her left, slowly sipped it then placed it gently back on the table. It wasn't until Troy reached for the rifle that she reacted. And it was so quick that if you asked anyone in the bar what they had seen none would be able to answer correctly.

The smell of hot metal filled the air as the temperature in the room suddenly rose by about thirty degrees. Still holding her cards in her right hand JP now held a flaming sword in her left hand just mere inches under Troy's throat.

It was so close that he could feel the hairs on his chin singeing off. The sweat now dripping down his chin evaporating before it could fall off.

"I stand corrected," Troy said.

"That is the rarest weapon in the universe, the Alverian flaming sword. A one-of-a-kind flaming sword, forged with the three rarest metals mixed with the sweat from a Blue Synge. A sword that once pulled from its sheath ignites and continues to heat up indefinitely. Ultimately making it hot enough to cut through anything. Thus the only way to quell the flames is by returning it to its sheath, which is also made of those same three metals."

The temperature in the room rose another twenty degrees causing many in to have trouble breathing.

"Hey, didn't I tell you not to get friendly with the natives?" Price asked.

"I wasn't. Technically I was trying to get friendly with the…" Troy started to say before he was interrupted by Price.

"Hasn't there been enough killing today? So just put it away."

JP finally looked up from her cards and turned slowly towards Devon, wondering who he thought he was ordering around. Though as she turned, she noticed the excited look on Troy's face and his big grin as he stared at her. Then out the corner of her eye, she noticed that her hair was glowing. It was at this point that she realized that the purple glow coming from underneath her hair was actually that of a small hand held plasma gun. And though her face didn't show it, for a moment she was shocked but that quickly turned to anger. Not because he might have reflexes that could be on par with hers. But because, up until that point, no one had ever gotten a weapon that close to her without her knowing and it really pissed her off.

The glow began to slowly fade as Troy took his finger off the trigger which brushed her hair slightly as he put it back in its holster. JP moved the sword away from his neck and with a couple of flicks of her wrist a bluish white streak cut through the air as she quickly placed the sword back in its sheath on her right thigh, next to her Plasma Whip.

Devon got up and walked over to her. As he did, he shot Troy a look. Troy then turned and walked out the door behind her.

Devon said,

"Sorry, he sometimes gets carried away especially when he sees a nice weapon. He just seems to not be able to stop at the appropriate time. But after seeing your skills I think that you'd be a good match for what we're looking for. Would you be interested in joining our team?" He asked.

"No." JP replied.

Just then, Troy poked his head back into the room.

"If she says no just, play on her love for rare weapons. Let her know about our jurisdiction and the salvage options we get. Also tell her that we could probably help her with finding the companion to that sword. You know the one that supposedly produces an infinite amount of cold that makes it possible to freeze and shatter anything it touches. The only weapon that could match that flaming sword of hers and that goes with that second sheath that she's got attached to the back of that rifle." Troy then smiled and disappeared out the door again.

"You're right," JP said,

"He doesn't know when to stop."

JP put her cards down and slowly got up from the table. It seemed that the rest of them were no longer interested in continuing the game. Especially with the small display that she put on earlier and she was still a little upset about the incident with Troy. She knew of Recon teams but none were known for their skills. She wondered what made him so different. More than that, was it just him or was the whole team skilled? Leaving the mercenary life was not something she had ever thought about but she was intrigued with the idea of finding that companion sword.

As she started to walk out of the room Devon said.

"Well we'll be here for a few more hours so if you change your mind, just let us know."

"I'll think about it," JP said as she walked out of the door.

Watching all of this, Nicki turned to the bartender and asked, "Do Recon teams usually recruit people like that?"

"No. Recon teams are usually made up of five members. Let's see, Pat over there is their enforcer. AJ is their medic. Devon is their leader and strategist. Troy is there for comic relief but I guess he's a pretty good pilot and weapons expert. And Granddad over there is their resident historian, language expert and sometimes diplomat. But he's been talking about retirement lately, so they may be trying to find a replacement for him." The bartender said while wiping off the counter.

~Diplomat and historian.~ she thought to herself.

Just then Troy walked by the door behind her. She turned and followed.

"Hey, can I ask you a question?" She shouted.

Captain Beckett and Lt. Heart could hear the sound of soft rain coming from nearby. They looked around for the source since that was the sort of thing the pure lyncers wouldn't normally create. Lightning and rain were not essential and held no purpose on this planet. When plant life and flowers, like everything else on the planet, could be controlled by mental thought then there would be no need for either. After a few moments they were able to find the source. To the left of them on the other side of the gravity fence, they saw a small red puddle beginning to form in the grass. It seemed to appear out of nowhere then it stopped. A few seconds later the slopping sound of what could only be described as meat falling on water, began coming from the same spot. Then small, three inch, grayish cubes began falling from about five feet in the air. Then everything became quiet as they both tried to comprehend what they had just witnessed. Then a few feet away another area of red rain appeared with three inch cubes falling into a pile on top of it. This appeared in about six different spots before finally ending.

"This makes no sense." Captain Beckett said.

"It does if you factor in the TDG," the Commander said.

"A TDG?" Captain Beckett asked curiously.

"What is a TDG?" Lt. Heart asked.

"Temporal Displacement Grenade," the Commander replied.

"There's no such thing, "the Captain interrupted.

"You really don't know what's going on, do you? Some expert you are."

The Lieutenant turned and looked at the Commander who smiled and said.

"The Temporal Displacement Grenade was something your former prisoner created. It was experimental back when I first heard of it, but seeing this means that it might have been perfected. One of the proposed uses was to be able to turn back time in order to bypass an unbeatable security system. So I'm sure you can guess what those puddles are."

"The Red Grid." Lt. Heart said.

The Captain couldn't believe what he just heard but with what he just witnessed, he came to the same conclusion.

"It should be safe to send your men in now." The Commander said.

Then turning to Lt. Heart, he said.

"We should head to the council chambers and see Price now."

The Commander walked into the council chambers and realized that somehow Specialist Keller had made it there before him. Councilor Price was the only council member there. He sat in the center chair behind a long curved desk that almost encompassed the entire back of the room. It was meant to seat thirteen but there were currently only twelve council members.

"Commander," Price said.

"Councilor," the Commander replied as he turned toward specialist Keller.

"So, another planet?" Price asked.

"You have my report," the Commander said.

"I'm sure the CSO has already briefed you and sent you the vid files that we recovered."

"Yes but that doesn't mean that the council still doesn't look at it as a chance to bring you up on charges," Price replied.

"They can do what they want, "the Commander replied, slightly raising his voice.

"I'm doing my job and if they don't like it...."

No one had noticed that Dr. Zynge {Zin-ge} had walked into the room through the door behind Nicki and the Commander. He stopped just short of walking between the two of them.

"And you always seem to get the job done. So they should really ease up on you." Dr. Z chimed in.

The Commander slowly turned to see the good doctor standing next to him and the smile slowly left his face. Specialist Keller could feel the mood quickly change. Suddenly it felt as if time had suddenly slowed. Not because she knew what was going to happen, though she and the Councilor should have seen it coming. No it was the look in the Commander's eyes. It was a look she had seen before. Only the one time, but once had been enough for her.

The Commander slowly turned and blood exploded from Dr. Z's nose. Nicki barely saw his fist recoil as he pulled it back.

The doctor had an average build but compared to the Commander he was small, so it was no surprise that the hit knocked him off of his feet. As the Commander brushed by Nicki, Councilor Price yelled for the guards.

Six council guards rushed in from the back of the room. Three from the door on the right and three from the door on the left. Which was now the direction that the Commander was facing as he straddled the doctor.

They all tackled him at once but not before the Commander was able to get in three more good hits.

It was no surprise that the Commander was able to throw the guards around the room like sacks of potatoes. Members of the DSU were at the top of the food chain, made up of former Recon and TET (Tactical Elimination Team) members. Below them were the military/security made up of those who couldn't get into the DSU. Lastly were the council guards.

Price was well aware of this but he needed to buy some time. He quickly tapped his wrist twice and called for security.

The Commander had become so enraged that he didn't notice that each time he threw off one of the guards that they took one of his weapons with them, placing them in a pile in front of the Councilor.

Moments later heavily armed security members entered the room. Two through the door on the right, two through the left and two from the door behind Councilor Price, who stood on either side of him.

"Ok that's enough of that!" Price yelled.

But the melee continued.

"Alright, I'm only going to give you a ten count and if he doesn't give up by then shoot Specialist Keller." Price said.

Security then raised their weapons and aimed them at Nicki. The Commander who was still struggling at the bottom of the pile wasn't sure if he had actually heard what Price had said. That was until the Councilor started counting.

Price began counting down.

"10...9...8.."

Though the Commander heard the countdown he was struggling even more, pissed that the Councilor would even consider doing something like this.

Price continued.

"7...6..5.."

And the fact that security would actually follow that order and point their weapons at his sis was unforgivable.

But Price kept going.

"4...3..."

"Ok..ok." The Commander gave in,

"You can stop now."

"2..." Price said

The Commander shouted as he stopped struggling.

"Devon!"

The council guard followed suit and when Price stopped counting the security officers lowered their weapons. The

Commander could barely see through the guards that stood around him but he could see the pile of weapons in front of the Councilor. He then realized that he had been totally disarmed.

Price had actually taken his advice. When they were younger, Troy always used to say,

"Skill doesn't last forever. So make sure to find someone worthy to pass your skills down to. "

It looked like he had. It's not that council guards aren't skilled, but to disarm a member of the DSU, without their knowledge, is a skill very few posses.

"It's over! You can put the gun down now," Price said.

There was no reply.

Price repeated himself a little louder this time,

"I said you can put that down now. Specialist Keller put the gun down!"

With all the commotion no one had seen the good doctor trying to sneak out the back. No one except for Nicki, who had pulled a gun, aimed it at the back of the Doctor's head and softly said,

"Where do you think you're going?"

"Commander," Price said,

"You'd better talk to your Sis before I continue the countdown."

The Commander pushed his way through the guards to see Nicki holding her weapon at the back of the good doctor's head, which was bad. Nicki didn't like guns and she especially didn't like using them, so for her to have her finger on the trigger of one wasn't good. Then panic set in as the Commander realized something. What if she figured it out? She had confirmed the Commander's findings when she saw the vid files he gave her. But what if she actually pieced together the whole thing and came to the same conclusion that he did? If so, the there'd be no way he could stop her from pulling that trigger.

"Hey Sis, can you take your finger off the trigger and put that down?" The Commander asked.

"Ok. 2!" Price shouted

"Nicki!" The Commander shouted.

Nicki quickly snapped out of it, slowly took her finger off the trigger and lowered her weapon. Dr. Z wiped the sweat from his face and let out a big sigh.

"Wow that was close. I thought you were actually going to let her do it. Guess you really do like this one, not like what's her name." Dr. Z said.

"Shut up," the Commander said under his breath.

"No really I mean you did let the last one suffer, a lot. What was her name?" He asked.

Now clinching his fist and gritting his teeth the Commander spoke a little louder this time.

"I said shut up."

"No really, I can't remember her name. You know the cute one with the dark hair. I mean you must remember her. Though I guess you didn't care for her at all, not like Specialist Keller here. I mean the way you let her suffer. Not only her but you even scarified your un-born..."

But the Commander interrupted him by shouting at the top of his lungs,

"I said shut up!"

The entire room then began to shake, startling everyone. The shaking began to intensify as the color of the Commanders eyes began to change. His pupils began shrinking until they were almost gone. They then began darting around his eyes moving so fast that it began to look as if three small red streaks were flowing around his eyes in three different directions.

The doctor became silent, not because the Commander had told him to but mainly because he couldn't breathe. He began gasping for air. Both arms by his sides began to shake violently.

Fractures appeared in the floor, walls and ceiling a couple of feet from the Commander, cascading towards the good doctor stopping just short of him. The color in the doctor's eyes began to fade and though his feet were still planted firmly on the ground the doctor began to slowly fall backwards. But to everyone's surprise he stopped when his body was at about a thirty degree angle from the floor.

It seems that the only one not in shock was Councilor Price who quickly sprang into action. He planted both hands on the desk and leaped over the table, reached down into the middle of the pile and pulled out a weapon. He aimed it at the back of the Commander's head and quickly squeezed the trigger three times. The room as well as the doctor stopped shaking. The Commander crumpled to the ground. Then the doctor hit the ground with a thud and gasped loudly as air began to rush back into his lungs. Nicki fell to her knees and began to cry. "He's dead! You killed him; I can't believe that you actually killed him!" Nicki screamed.

Councilor Price turned and handed the weapon to the nearest guard and said,

"He's not dead."

Nicki, still with tears running down her face slowly looked up at the Councilor.

"He's not dead. With all the years you've known him do you actually think that he'd die that easily, especially by my hands?" Councilor Price asked her.

The Councilor then motioned to one of the security officers to take the weapon away from Specialist Keller while she was still distracted. Then turning back to the guard he said, "Please put this weapon in the Council's Vault. Make sure to mark it Eastern Research Facility."

The guard, not recognizing the weapon asked what it was.
Councilor Price said, "That's an N.L.C. (Neuro Lync Cutter).
Originally known as the Mental Lync Disrupter. But more
commonly known as The Night Night Gun."

The N.L.C is actually one of the few weapons banned in
their society. When the crime of Mental Fetal Lyncing
originally sprung up, a device was quickly developed to
counteract it. It was meant to quickly stop the linc and it did,
like running into a wall at a hundred miles an hour quick.
Which, not only caused severe pain but also rendered the
person unconscious for a minimum of three days, which no one
seemed to mind. Although another side effect was that not only
did it cut the lync with the fetus it would slowly cut the linc
between the person's brain and the rest of his body. If a mental
stimulant wasn't introduced within a short period of time, he
would eventually stop breathing. Which again, no one seemed
to mind. Unfortunately, an unforeseen side effect was that
when the child was born he or she would remember the mental
violation they suffered. Not only that, but it was found that
they experienced and remembered the pain from the linc being
cut, which no one was ok with. So the device was banned. All
were destroyed with the exception of one which was kept at the
Eastern Research Facility.

The guard recognized the name and was surprised that the
Commander would walk around with a banned weapon like

that. But it was more surprising that the Councilor not only knew how to use the weapon but in the heat of the moment was able to find it, in the middle of a pile of weapons, quickly raise it up, aim it and hit his mark like it was nothing.

The color was slowly coming back to Dr. Z's eyes and his breathing began to normalize.

Councilor Price began to walk back around the desk; he tapped his wrist twice and said, "Medical to council chambers, we have an N.L.C. situation."

Two guards helped Specialist Keller to her feet. Two began to gather up the Commander's weapons and the last two attended to Dr. Z. "Please escort the doctor to the detention area and make sure you let them know he's now considered an Omega Level threat, Level One." Councilor Price told the guards.

The remaining five security officers then helped to escort Dr. Z to the detention area.

When the Commander came to a week had gone by. He slowly raised his hand and rubbed the back of his head. There was no bruise but he felt a strange sensation, almost as though there was pressure building up in the back there. Maybe it was more like a small throbbing sensation but he wasn't sure which. He knew something was off but just couldn't put his finger on it.

Councilor Price walked in and headed towards him, "Does it hurt?" he asked.

"No but it doesn't feel right maybe because I thought I heard someone mention that Dr. Z is still alive?" the Commander replied.

"Yes that's right. The council decided to impose a different punishment. One that would better suit him."

"You're making a big mistake," the Commander said. "You should end him now while you have the chance. Destroy his lab, experiment and notes while you're at it."

"The Council decided that that wouldn't be in our best interest. We might need his expertise again at some point." Price replied.

The Commander, still rubbing his head, shook it slightly said,

"Something just doesn't feel right."

"Sorry but it was the only way. The council wanted to label you an Omega Level Threat as well but I was able to convince then not to. Though it did come at a high price." Price informed him.

The Commander stopped rubbing his head and looked at Price.

"They put a chip in your head." Price said

The look on the Commander's face changed drastically.

"Don't worry, it's not one of the good doctor's inventions and it's been upgraded to the last model." Price added.

Which didn't change the look on the Commander's face. But Price continued,

"It's a regulator to keep your M.L.P under control. We still don't know the full extent of what Dr. Z did to you on Atavus but we do know that the incident in the council chambers registered off the charts at the CSO. The discomfort should go away in a few days. Now just a few things, the regulator is set at thirty five percent."

The Commander said.

"What? Why the...."

But Price cut the Commander short and continued,

"Calm down and let me explain. Like I mentioned earlier, it was the only way that they wouldn't consider you an Omega Level threat. The chip is set at thirty five percent because they don't know your full potential and they want to make sure there's no repeat of what happened in the council chambers. Now unlike your military linc this one is linked directly to the Eastern Research Facility and you really don't want to tamper with it because it has a small charge in it. So if you try to adjust it, remove it or tamper with it in any way, it'll blow."

"How small are we talking?" The Commander asked,

"Headache small or you won't need to buy hats anymore small?"

"Small like Rylone {rye-lawn}," Price answered.

Rylone was the first mission that members of Recon 15 went on when they first joined the DSU. Pat had said that he was going to use a small charge to break into one of the facilities they were scoping out. Though, to this day people say that you can actually still see the crater from space.

"So they just want to run a few more tests on you before releasing you back to active duty." Price said as he turned to walk away.

Specialist Keller started to walk into the room as the Commander began to sit up. He swung his legs over the bed and said,

"You know you and the Council have done so much for me that I feel I owe you. So I'm going to say something to you that I've never said before and you can share this with the rest of the Council. I quit!"

He then began reaching for the Omega/DSU patch on his arm. Councilor Price stopped dead in his tracks as did Specialist Keller.

"Did you hear that?" Price said looking at Specialist Keller. "You can't quit. But you know that. I mean you helped write the Displacers Act and part of the code of conduct for the DSU, so quitting is not an option."

The Commander stopped and began to move his hand away from the patch.

"You know, you're right." The Commander said before pausing.

"But I can give you my Notice of Intent."

"Notice of Intent?" Price asked with a puzzled look on his face. "What is that even supposed to mean? I mean, that doesn't even make sense."

"It doesn't," the Commander said,

"which is partially how I was able to sneak it into the Displacer's Act without anyone really noticing. Because yes, you're correct in the fact that I can't quit. But the Displacer's Act also states that anyone in the DSU, who has reached the rank of Commander and who has witnesses, been a part of or enacted at least twenty Omega Level threats, can give their Notice of Intent which allows them to leave the DSU, no questions asked and no reprisals or retaliations shall be leveled against them in any way. Anyone who did would also be subject to the penalties of the Displacer Act. It can be given in written or verbal form. The only requirement is that it has to be done in front of the entire council or the highest ranking council member and a member of the DSU has to be present at the time."

The Commander then hopped out of the bed and began walking towards Price with a big grin on his face. As he reached the Councilor, he tore off his patch and threw it down at his feet and continued walking out the door.

The Commander walked into the council chambers with Lt. Heart behind him. Again Councilor Price was the only one present. He looked up and said,

"Commander."

"Councilor." The Commander responded as he looked around the room.

"Never thought I'd step foot in here again."

"Well, we have a situation and I need you to check something…." Price said

The Commander interrupted before Price could continue, "He's gone."

"We don't know that. But I need you to go check to see…"

But the Commander interrupted him again.

"I said he's gone and I'm going home now."

"That's impossible. It was probably some glitch, which is why I need you to…."

But this time it was Lt. Heart who interrupted,

"Sorry to interrupt but the Commander insisted that we stop there first and we saw…." She paused then continued, "Something. I don't know what happened there but the Commander could be right."

"So like I said, I'm going home now." The Commander said.

"Hold on a second. If it's true then we really do have a problem." Councilor Price said intensively.

"What do you mean we?" the Commander asked.

"Well you're responsible for his capture, so don't you think that getting even with you or Specialist Keller might be first on his list?" Price asked.

"Doubt that," the Commander said.

"Remember I tried to end him and you stopped me. She tried to also and I stopped her. But you and the Council came up with that ingenious punishment especially for him, so don't you think that you and the Council would be top on his list instead of me and my Sis? So like I said, this doesn't concern me."

"Fine, what do you want?" Price asked.

"Nothing. There's nothing that you can offer me to go after him." The Commander replied.

"What do you want!?" He said more sternly.

"Like I said…."

"Whatever you want, just ask." Price interrupted.

"Ok, how about you have them take this chip out of my head?" the Commander asked.

"That I can't do." He replied

"Then we're done here" the Commander said as he turned and started to walk away adding.

"Good luck."

"Wait, I can talk to the council and see if they'd be willing to lessen the restrictions and up your M.L.P. to about…" Councilor Price said as he thought of a number.

The Commander stopped, turned around and said, "Ok, let me, stop you right there. We both know that the only way I'd do this is if the chip is taken out. And since that's off the table, it means that you already talked to the Council and got them to agree to something that you think would change my mind. So don't play, just give me the final offer or I walk." Councilor Price smiled and said, "Guess we've know each other too long to play games. Fine, they agreed to up your M.L.P. to fifty percent. With the possibility of more once the mission is complete. Oh and that means bringing him back alive."

Looking annoyed the Commander said, "Ok, well if you want him back alive then I'll agree to the first part but you have to remove the chip if I complete the mission. Take that to the Council and let me know what they say. Also I need you to turn off whatever mental blocking field you have on the facility. In the mean time, I'll be heading home." "Why do you need the field off at the facility?" Price asked. "Because the only way I can track him is to use something I have stashed away down there. So go check with the Council and let me know if we have a deal." The Commander said. "Deal." He said.

"And since you've been out of the DSU for so long, we've already picked a few of your team members for you."

The Commander turned around and just stared at the Councilor. Looks like he had still held out on him he thought, but there was nothing that he could do about it now, especially if he wanted that chip out.

Looking down at his desk Price said,

"So Lt. Heart is first on the list. Followed by Captain Beckett, whom I assume you met earlier." He then tapped his wrist twice and said.

"What about you? I know you've been listening in on this. So do you want in on this mission or are you going to sit this one out?" Price asked.

Crystal's voice came out of his Lync and said,

"Well I can't exactly let the Commander go on this mission with a team of people that he doesn't know.

So I'm in."

"Ok," Price said, "Lastly, I was thinking…"

The Commander interrupted,

"Hold on. I don't want Specialist Keller involved in this one."

"Ok," Councilor Price said,

"well then I'll have to find a fifth member for you."

"No, that's ok. I have someone in mind that'd be perfect for this," The Commander said.

"Ok, well head down to medical for the adjustment then you can go round up all your team members." Price ordered.

The Commander headed towards medical while Lt. Heart stayed behind to talk with the Councilor. She would eventually meet back up with the Commander on his way out.

When they finally met up again the Commander looked at the Lt. and said,

"Sorry but it looks like you've been drafted also."

"No," she said, "actually I volunteered."

"Now why would you do a thing like that?" the Commander asked.

"I mean I'd un-volunteer in a minute if I could."

The Lieutenant still couldn't believe that this was the same man who was once the most revered man in the DSU. The one who actually co-created the DSU. especially after what he had just said.

The two of them headed back to GF1 and met up with Captain Beckett. As they arrived the scene was a lot less chaotic than when they left. The bodies had all been removed but there were still red puddles in the grass. They met up with Beckett inside.

"Looks like we're back," the Commander said with a smile.

"And I hear you've been drafted into our little gang also."

Captain Beckett just stared at him then said,

"I'm only coming along to make sure the prisoner comes back in the same condition he left."

"Oh you mean in pieces?" the Commander asked. "And don't you mean, former prisoner?"

Captain Beckett just continued staring at him eventually stating,

"The Council wants to make sure that you bring the fugitive back alive. They said that you two have history. Something about you and your former teammate being permanently mentally lynced to each other because of him. So I guess that female voice earlier wasn't an AI after all."

"No, that was Crystal and she'll be joining us on this mission." The Commander replied.

"So where's the fifth member of the group?" Captain Beckett asked.

"We'll pick him up along the way but first," the Commander said, as he walked through the large white room past where Dr. Z had been kept.

He headed towards the back left corner of the room then stopped and looked around. He looked down at the floor then up at the ceiling and then stared at the spot where the two walls meet. As he put a hand on each wall and pushed he said,

"This is the spot, right?"

"Yes," Crystal said aloud.

The Commander then knelt down and tried to put his right hand flat on the floor with his thumb right where the two walls met but he could only get his finger tips down.

"Guess they really didn't want anyone to go back down there. Well I hope this is enough," he said as he held his hand there for a moment then pressed as hard as he could.

A faint voice could be heard coming from underneath the floor.

"Verifying....verifying......verif......Access granted, welcome back Commander."

The Commander then stood up and took a couple steps back. Spots on the floor, starting at the corner of the wall, slowly began to disappear but nothing was underneath. It was as though the floor had just turned black. The Commander walked over and stood right where the floor disappeared. He stopped, turned around and said,

"You coming?"

Captain Beckett and Lt. Heart joined him. Once they were all in position they were quickly lowered down into the darkness below until even the light above them had disappeared. Eventually a dim light appeared from beneath them until it engulfed them revealing the once abandoned Displacer's base. And as the platform finally reached the bottom, a male voice echoed all around them.

"Welcome back Commander. It's been….actually it seems that I am no longer connected to any outside systems so I'm not actually sure when you last accessed my systems."

"It's ok," the Commander said,

"I haven't been connected to an outside system for a long time either. But we're just here to pick something up."

Lt. Heart and Captain Beckett followed the Commander through the large facility. Where they were now made the facility above it look small in comparison. Though the place had been empty for years there wasn't a speck of dirt or dust anywhere. They finally arrived at the hanger but it was empty. "Was there supposed to be something here?" Captain Beckett asked.

The Commander ignored him and said,

"Yeah, looks like they finally installed it after I left. Not sure why since no one has used this since I left. Crystal, if you would?"

Crystal lynced to the ship then there was a large shimmer in the visual spectrum as the ship appeared before them. Once the ship de-cloaked the hatch opened and the engines began to cycle up.

"Looks like the ship's armory is fully stocked," Crystal announced.

"Guess we can head out then." The Commander replied.

They boarded the ship and headed towards the bridge as the hatchway closed behind them. Just like the facility there was no dust anywhere in the ship. Even the air seemed fresh, like it had been cycled out recently.

As they settled in on the bridge Crystal began doing a systems check.

"Looks like there have been a number of upgrades since we last used her. Besides the cloak, the weapons system has been upgraded and it even looks like they took out the sub-light engine and added some kind of hyper-drive engine in its place." She said.

"Nice. Well I guess it's time to open it up and take her out," the Commander replied.

Then the Commander pushed a button on the console. Outside, in a large grassy area behind the facility the ground began to violently shake as a large portion of the ground began to open up. Inside light from above began to shine in on the far side of the hanger as a small amount of condensation began to fall from the mixing of the air. The ship began to slowly move towards the hangar opening. Once underneath, it stopped and hovered.

"Systems check complete. Ready for takeoff." Crystal announced.

"Take her out." The Commander commanded.

Suddenly the ship shot straight up in the air before quickly coming to a halt a few hundred yards above the facility. It happened so fast that they almost blacked out. Even Captain Beckett who had been on many a mission felt a little queasy after that.

"Sorry about that," Crystal said,

"the engines arc a bit touchy. And this is the first time dealing with this new drive system. But I think I have it now. Heading out."

The ship began to ascend straight up but at a more respectable speed this time. They stopped just outside the orbital Quarantine Station, gently spun around it and headed out of the system.

"What happened to picking up the fifth member?" Captain Beckett asked.

"Oh don't worry, well meet up with him soon," the Commander answered,

"Crystal, is the file still intact?"

"Yes sir,' she replied,

"Looks like no one has attempted to access it since I logged it in."

"Good, then wait till we're at least a couple of galaxies away and then send the signal. Time to cash in that favor." He said.

As the ship sped off, the Commander really only had one thought on his mind. ~This time I will end him!~

Next time......The Displacers

ATAVUS: Scream of the Unborn

About the Author

I'll start this description by using one of Mr. Baker's favorite quotes, "What if Stephen King, Clive Barker or John Carpenter had never written a story or movie script in their lifetime? What if Charles Manson, Jeffery Dahmer or the Son of Sam had?"

Now that should say a lot. But if you want to know more, then I'll continue.

Born in Hartford, Ct. Mr. Baker now resides in the Springfield, Ma. area. A baker by trade, he is also a standup comedian, a song writer and with this now an author as well.

Mr. Baker loves anime, so much so that most would call him an "Otaku" he wouldn't but most people who know him would. He grew up a fan of all things horror and sci-fi related and literally owns close to 1000 movies and TV shows, almost all of them sci-fi related. And yes most are on VHS but he assures me that he has at least five different devices still capable of playing them. With watching so many movies that started off great but had terrible endings, he dreamt of starting a company in which people would hire him just to write a good ending for their movies, though this was pre internet. But coming up with so many different movie endings, with no real way to reach out to Hollywood, ultimately lead him to start writing his own unique stories that he'd now like to share.

With this first book, Mr. Baker said that he tried to combine his love for sci-fi with his love for how some of his favorite anime stories were told with a dash of comedy on top.

And as the reader he hopes that you'll let him know if he succeeded or not.